In The Land of Keldarra...

Marrida and Alagur

Nathalie M.L. Römer

ISBN-13: 9789188459015

Emerentsia Publications
Marielundsvägen 9c
711 95 Gusselby
Sweden
emerentsiabooks.com

Ordering Information:

Orders by U.S. trade bookstores and wholesalers. Please contact Ingram: One Ingram Blvd., La Vergne, TN 37086 • 615.793.5000 or visit www.ingramcontent.com.

Independently printed as a Swedish publication.

Interior design and layout by Emerentsia Publications.

Official Website:
nathaliemlromer.com

Official Facebook Page:
facebook.com/nathaliemlromer

Official Twitter Account:
twitter.com/nmlromer

Book website: nathaliemlromer.com/marrida-and-alagur

For my loving partner Anders.

Marrida

CHAPTER ONE

Marrida rushes through the street. She's late. She was told to *be* at the door of the Temple of Ruh'nar at midday exactly, and of all days to be late, she is late today. She already pictures the stern frown on the Elder's face on arriving. She already imagines that she would get told to go home, that they reject her, and all because she's late.

It's sixteen days earlier the Elder came to see her uncle to be allowed to do *The Test* on Marrida. Marrida still chuckles at the idea of her stern uncle being told what to do by this mysterious old woman...

Marrida stops walking for a moment to catch her breath. She sees puffs of breaths escape her mouth into the cool early spring air. She giggles and blows a few times to make the same puffs of cloud appear.

I'll walk slow for a while. I want to feel like nothing matters for longer...

Going to this Temple won't be the same as going to the school she attended for four days every other third day. It's somewhere people went when they are past their First Rites…

But mine is in three seasons. How can I even be able to go to the Temple this young?

Most of the last five years, ever since the women arrived to do The Test, was strange to Marrida. It seems to her that their arrival made her uncle become moody. However, he started doing a lot more stuff with Marrida and her younger brother and sister. But it seems now that the fun would stop now she's going to the Temple.

"Marrida…"

She turns and sees her sister Kalisa rushing to her. "What are you doing out here?" she calls out. "You know you're too young to be on the streets alone…"

"Esbara is coming too," Kalisa pants heavily, "He's just so slow…"

Marrida looks up, just as Esbara turns a corner.

"What are you doing out here?" she asks again, this time asking Esbara.

"Huh what?" he mumbles, "She wanted to go, she pretty much dragged me out of the house…"

"Why?" Marrida asks.

"I wanted to see the Temple," Kalisa grins at her older sister looking down at her.

"But you can't go inside. It's forbidden…" Marrida says.

"Why?" Kalisa asks, imitating her sister's voice. Marrida stares at Kalisa with an annoyed frown. She loves her little sister, but sometimes Kalisa is just way too annoying to be nice.

"Because it's not allowed," she says, "If you want to look, do it from the other end of the square, so she doesn't see you."

"She?" Kalisa asks.

"Elder Sharriba. She's the one in charge, and she seems rather stern…" Marrida says.

"But you said she's nice…" Kalisa says.

"She's also the leader there. I don't know… I've only met her once, and she was nice when I met her, but Uncle Joharan seems to think she is--" Marrida begins to say. She pauses for a moment, then says. "She was nice to me. Uncle doesn't seem to like her…"

Marrida bends forward until her face is in front of Kalisa's face.

"Go ask Uncle Joharan yourself *why* he doesn't like her," She grins when her sister's face shows shock, then a bit of fear.

Kalisa stares at her sister. "You're being mean…"

"Oh, am I…?" Marrida says. "Well then, that means *no* sweet biscuits for you after the evening meal, when I'm home again."

"Why are you being so mean to her?" Esbara asks. "She's done nothing to you. She wanted to see you go inside, I do too, by the way…"

"Suits yourself, but stay out of the way, so you don't embarrass me…" Marrida says.

She turns and starts walking briskly, the mood for a slow walk all but evaporated from her mind. It's now replaced with the other thought that wants to keep invading her mind.

Somehow, I don't think I'm going to the Temple to be a Keeper. Somehow, I keep feeling today is the beginning of a future I never asked for.

The thought worries Marrida.

She glances occasionally to see if her sister and brother are still following her, or that they've got bored and returned home. But they follow her. They seem to want to keep pace, so they're out of earshot of her, so she can't speak or call out to them without drawing attention to herself. When Marrida glances for the fourth time behind, she catches her brother pulling Kalisa back, essentially preventing her from walking any faster than he makes her go.

Marrida glares at Esbara, who seems to ignore her stare. She stops walking and makes it obvious from her posture she wants them near.

"I'm just going there to be a Temple Maiden if you want to

know it. Uncle Joharan said that's why they did *that* thing when they came. Elder Sharriba said only those who are pure can be one," she says softly, "Now you know a secret, Kalisa, so please don't embarrass me there, or I'll be sent away, alright?"

Kalisa nods, then she gives one more hard stare, then gives Marrida a hug. "Hope you get to be one..." Kalisa whispers.

Marrida walks towards where the other girls, and some women, are lining up for the doors of the Temple to open.

She's late, but as she steps in behind a group of women, who all seem to know one another, they immediately throw disapproving glances her way before they giggle.

Marrida sees a few other girls rushing towards the lineup.

It seems something like sixty girls and women stand there now. It's obvious to her she's there as the youngest...

"So then, how come *you* are here? Are you lost?"

Marrida looks towards the direction where the question came and sees an older girl staring at her. Marrida guesses she's around twenty and may have done her Second Rites recent.

"No, I'm here because I did The Test," she replies, then looks towards where her sister and brother stand. She sees Esbara frown, and she wonders why he frowns instead of being happy about seeing her go inside.
"Oh, so they let the 'children' in now too..." the older girl says.
"I'm not a child..." Marrida replies.
"Have you done First Rites yet?" the older girl asks.
"I'm doing it in three seasons from now, and--" Marrida says.
"So you're a child..." the older girl interjects, then laughs loud, before she continues, "Look here, we got a child here to give us some fun when things get *too* boring in there for us..."

Marrida glares at the woman.

"Just so you remember it, *child*, my name is Sarayna..." comes the retort as the woman glares at Marrida maliciously.

CHAPTER TWO

Marrida ignores the older girl speaking to her and concentrates instead on the person who'd come to the doors to welcome the new people joining the Temple. "Please, come inside as fast as you can. Don't leave us waiting…"

I'm one of them, regardless of what the older girl in front of me said.

Marrida cranes her neck to see past the crowd. The voice isn't of the woman who came to her uncle's house, so Marrida guesses that she, Elder Sharriba, is waiting inside.

Marrida wonders if she'll really be the way as she described to her siblings. She glances sidelong and sees her siblings wave the moment they catch her eye. She waves back, grinning.

I guess it can't be that bad. Even if the idiot in front of me is being nasty. Why is she so nasty towards me, anyway?

Marrida looks around her as she walks into the vestibule of the Temple. She's seen nothing as expansive as this. She knows the building is big from walking past it for as long as she can remember, but it seems so much bigger now she saw the inside. She cranes her neck to see if she sees the mysterious Elder Sharriba, but gives up after a few minutes, and glances back towards the square, and waves at her siblings one more time.

Then she sees the doors closing, so waves once more, but this time a *"Go home"* motion. She turns to see what goes on inside the Temple and realises the other people present seem to be taken to different rooms, following one or two women. Once the last group leaves, which includes the rather annoying woman called Sarayna, Marrida finds herself standing alone in the middle of the vestibule.

For a moment, she wonders if she's about to be sent home for one reason or another. She hears soft footsteps coming from somewhere…

"I hope you remember me…"

Marrida looks up to see the woman she met several years earlier, standing in front of her. She still wears her silver-grey hair tied back, like when she came to visit Marrida's uncle, or more precisely her.

"Yes, I do…" Marrida says, suddenly feeling shy.

She fidgets and moves her foot from side to side, hoping her movements won't get noticed.

"Come with me. We'll sit down to talk for a while. My name is Sharriba. When we're alone, you can call me *that*, but when anyone else is present, you have to address me as Elder Sharriba, understood?" she says.

Marrida nods.

"Come…"

Elder Sharriba turns and walks up the stairway. Marrida follows her after one moment more of feeling shy. Then curiosity becomes greater than her shyness, and she walks behind the Elder up the stairway.

At the top, they turn left in a long corridor and walk until they get to a door. Sharriba opens it, then steps aside and motions for Marrida to walk in too. Marrida stares in awe at her surroundings. Everywhere she looks, she sees bookcases with books of every size and thickness.

There are a few women sitting at some tables, who glance up to see who entered the library.

It's obvious to Marrida they sit back down because the Elder motions at them to do so. They return to whatever work they're doing without even asking about her.

"They're the Keepers, well some of them at least," Elder says softly, "Come, we'll sit down in the corner there…"

Marrida sees Elder Sharriba point to a corner to her left.

"Sit down here," Sharriba motions at a chair. Marrida does as she's told, and looks shyly at the Elder, who sits down opposite of her, and smiles at Marrida, and suddenly she feels less shy, so she smiles back.

"Do you remember what I told you all those years ago when I came to visit your uncle's workshop?" Sharriba asks, "What I said about *not* telling what goes on in this building…"

Marrida nods.

"I have told no one…" she says, "Not even my brother and sister…"

"Good…" Sharriba says. "Those rules apply as of *this* day. But, before you can learn to be a Keeper, First Rites must be performed…"

"Why am I here then?" Marrida asks, then she blushes because she feels she spoke out of turn.

"You're officially a Temple Maiden until First Rites, but I'll personally start your learning," Sharriba states. "It's rather essential you start as soon as possible so I'm complying with the wishes of your mother…"

"My mother…" Marrida says, feeling shocked now.

"Yes, she specifically asked me one season before Kalisa's birthing to allow *you* to join the Temple. I said I couldn't let you join any earlier than when you're *one* year away from First Rites," Sharriba says. "You would have joined sooner, but we had the attack from the Wolf Riders a few months ago, and I wanted to wait until the city is calmer again…"

"I didn't know my mother knew about this place," Marrida says. "I thought only Keepers or future Keepers knew about it."

"A future Keeper is called an Acolyte, and *yes*, she knew about this place, because she once was a Keeper herself."

Marrida sits staring with her mouth open wide in shock at the revelation.

"So, if my mother came to ask for me to come here, it means

she made you a guardian for me too," Marrida says softly, "Uncle Joharan said he wasn't my only guardian…"

"That's true," Sharriba replies, "He knows I'm your other guardian. He and I decided *not* to tell you this information in a conversation shortly after your parents died. We decided it was better for you to know about me until it was time…"

Marrida stares incredulously at the floor for a few minutes.

"Why wouldn't my uncle tell me that?" Marrida asks, feeling angry now. "I had no one call a mother. I wanted someone to talk to, who understands how it is to be a girl. I miss my mother…"

Marrida cries. She hiccups a sob every few minutes. She leans on the table. Suddenly she feels an arm around her…

Marrida looks up at the Elder, who smiles back at her, concerned. "I think I know how you feel, even if I can't tell you why or how," Sharriba says, "Your mother asked me to look after you, so I can be the mother, and perhaps the friend that you want so much…"

Marrida nods and wipes the tears from her face. "I'm not even sure why I'm here," she says, "I feel like I don't belong here. Everyone is so much older…"

"You belong here because your mother wanted you to *be* here, and because I want you here, too," Sharriba says, "I know you won't understand it yet, but there will come a day when you'll know why you're here…"

CHAPTER THREE

Marrida sits staring through one of the few windows present in Elder Sharriba's room, and she sits staring wide-eyed at the gardens the massive walls of the Temple enclose. It seems to her the garden is so large, that part of it is actually shaded by the walls beyond.

She wonders if the Elder would permit her to walk in the garden…

Marrida hears footsteps approach and quickly sits down on the chair where the Elder told her to sit before she left the room. The door opens, and the Elder walks in carrying a large pitcher with a hot brew, and Marrida can smell its sweet smells in wafts drifting in her direction.

"I think you'll enjoy this tea," Sharriba says softly as she hands a cup of the brew to Marrida, who nods, then inhales to let the smell get deep into her nostrils.

"This smells good…"

"It is one of my favourite teas," Sharriba says, "So, now shall we talk more about what you're going to do here…"

Marrida nods a little, then swallows hard. She isn't entirely sure what she could do *here*.

"As you know, those who join, *first* are a Temple Maiden. That's a training position, where you help with the functioning of the Temple," Sharriba explains, "It will involve a lot of duties, some of which is for you to learn. Normally, it's rather limited in how much you learn, until you become an Acolyte. The reason I asked to see you privately, is that I want you to start that Acolyte training *now*… even though, the rules here usually forbid it. It's honouring your mother's wishes, why I'm going to do this. But you cannot tell anyone here, or at home, we've made this arrangement…"

Marrida nods, then she frowns before asking, "Why am I going to learn the stuff if I'm not the right age for it?"

"Because there are things going to happen when you'll need this," Sharriba says. "But let's get going with the first lessons rather than all this talk…"

Marrida is puzzled about the Elder's reaction.

She's certain the Elder gave her a clue about something that will happen to her but guesses the Elder isn't able to say much about it because of some sort of promise to her mother.

"Can I ask something about my mother?"

"Of course you can, but remember that I know little about your mother. I only know what she has told me, and what I know of your family from your uncle," Sharriba says, before sipping from her tea. While she does this, she cautiously looks at the girl who was placed in her charge in such unusual circumstances.

She knows what she knows, but is certain it isn't anything she can talk about with this girl. She has her own secrets to keep, and even though she feels certain this girl can be trusted with the information, she needs to do it in the right way and at the right time. She has a way to get the girl involved in what's going, and one day it will come…

"I know my mother is from Marridina, but I know nothing else about her really," Marrida says. "I know my parents became life partners after just one day. My father was in Marridina for trading when he met my mother…"

Sharriba looks up and is somewhat surprised by the comment. She didn't know the bonding between the girl's parents happened that fast. She immediately also feels a sharp pain go through her heart, because of the missed opportunity for love that passed her by because circumstance never permitted it to come to her.

"I was aware they were life partners soon after meeting, I didn't know that soon…" Sharriba says softly.

"My uncle told me about it, but mother and I also talked about it a year or so before she died," Marrida says, and Sharriba notes how the girl tries to make sure she keeps her emotions in check.

"I don't much about them, but what I *do* know I'll share with you," Sharriba says, and she notices that the promise seems to cheer the girl up.

"I'm somewhat familiar with Marridina, so I can tell you a *few* things about the region," Sharriba adds after a pause, "Maybe telling you more about the place she was from, will help you understand your mother and her origins more. Perhaps, it will give you information that helps you later…"

Marrida nods.

"You'll be a Keeper one day. When you become one, you'll have learnt the skills to recall this conversation and those with your mother, and that will help you find more answers about *who* your mother was…"

Marrida nods, but deep down she vows to learn the skills fast, so she can see the things about her mother she missed so much each day of her life.

"But, let me tell you more of your mother, or at least the information I know…" Sharriba smiles encouragingly when Marrida lifts her head and looks up at her.

"I sometimes dream of her, and of another woman, and I think it's my grandmother," Marrida says, "She's really old, has silver-white hair, and she smiles whenever I see her in the dream…"

"Dreams are powerful tools for us. More powerful than you know right now. One day, I'll teach you how to understand the meaning of them…"

"So, me dreaming about her, and that other woman, who seems to be my grandmother, has some sort of meaning…?"

"A dream isn't always certain," Sharriba says, "Sometimes, you need to learn its meaning in *many* dreams before you understand the complete message it wants to tell. If ever a person came to you, telling you he or she had a dream, do *not* dismiss it, but listen to *that* person so you can help them understand the dream…"

Marrida considers the Elder's words. "I'll try to remember it…" Marrida says after a few minutes, and she smiles at Sharriba.

"You mother came to Ruh'nar after she bonded as life partner with your father…" Sharriba continues.

"How old was she when it happened…?"

"I think she was a few years younger than your father, Markalo. You know your father and his brother Joharan are many years apart in age…?"

Marrida nods.

"Eshara came to the city as a stranger, and I don't think your uncle accepted her immediately. There were… reasons for that which I cannot explain you'd have to ask your uncle about it…"

"I'm not sure he wants to talk about stuff like that with me…" Marrida says hesitantly.

"Maybe not but there will be a day you must speak with him," Sharriba smiles weakly, and she thinks, *Maybe that will be what I will have to do one day…*

CHAPTER FOUR

Marrida meanders behind the Elder. She isn't sure where they're going. They stop at a door, and the Elder pulls a key from a small pouch she carries on her belt.

"You begin in your training in the room beyond this door," Sharriba says softly, "It's where I started my training when I arrived here so many years ago…"

Marrida frowns a moment, "What are you teaching me?" she asks.

"More than most here will learn, but remember you cannot tell anyone about this," Sharriba says sternly, "Much depends on what you learn here, more than you can even grasp right now…"

Marrida nods, and she stares at the door, now with heightened anticipation, wondering what's behind it. A few minutes later, she stands looking in awe at the small room, which seems very well used.

"This is my private chamber," Sharriba says softly, "You can sit there…"

Sharriba points at a low bench next to the narrow window. Marrida sits down, but is distracted by what she sees in the room… books and more books.

The Elder smiles as she sees Marrida's eyes dart from book to book.

I think I know a way to get her to learn to be a Keeper, and much more, and she won't even realise she's learnt it all, until she's many years older, Sharriba thinks, then she smiles at the delight the books seem to give the girl, before she asks, "Do you want to see something you'll use soon enough?"

She reaches up and removes a necklace from her neck. Marrida's eyes fly open. She never saw any gem that looks that pretty.

"They call this a Stone of Truth. It's the tool by which a Keeper can see images from the past," Sharriba says, "In normal circumstances, you'd only learn about this gem in two or even three years from now."

Sharriba pauses a moment, then continues explaining. "However, there's something you *must* remember at all times. No one, not your uncle, not your brother or sister, may know about these gems. Also, what I'm going to teach would be against the way they do things in the Order of Truth, so tell no other Temple Maiden, Acolyte, or even a Keeper of these additional teaching I *do* here. There are… things, reasons… you don't know about yet, but that will come to your life one day. This additional know I'm going to teach is crucial for you later…"

Marrida stares incredulously at the Elder. She nods, but she can't believe what she hears: that the Elder seems to go against the rules of her own Order to teach her these skills. She nods ever so slightly. She doesn't want it to appear she is so ready to go along with the idea. But already her mind is racing.

If she can learn this skill well, perhaps she can use it to see more of her mother's life before…

Marrida places her hand over the gem in Sharriba's hand on the Elder's instruction. The next thing she senses is darkness and something else…

What am I seeing? This is not Sharriba's room. Is this what she was talking about when she explained what the gem does…?

Marrida sees a woman, and the woman is familiar. The woman turns and smiles, and a shocked Marrida realises who she sees.

Mother…

Blackness, and then she's looking up at the Elder's face. "What happened…?" she asks hesitantly.

"You experienced a vision. You did one about your mother," Sharriba says gently, "The first time is always disorientating…"

"It went all black," Marrida says, and Sharriba notes an edge of panic to the girl's voice.

"That's normal," Sharriba places a reassuring hand against the girl's cheek.

"Will it be like that every time?"

"No, just the first few times can be disorienting. After you get in the practice, it will get easier to do a vision, and later it will be very easy. Almost effortless I'd say…" Sharriba explains.

"Was it like this for you the first time?" Marrida asks hesitantly.

"Yes, and I felt afraid because it was so unusual and--" Sharriba says. Marrida notices immediately the Elder wants to say more, but that she stops short of the full explanation why.

"I'll tell you one day when I can," Sharriba says, "I'll tell you when the time is right…"

Marrida frowns for a moment, then nods, *I guess I am too young to know*, she thinks.

"Is there any significance to what you see in a vision?"

"There *is*. You're watching events from the past. It helps you determine how the circumstances in the world exist." Sharriba explains.

"Can I see future things with it too?"

"*No*, but once there were some who *could* do it, but none exist anymore. None of them is around anymore…"

"Why is that?" Marrida asks, but her question remains unanswered.

"Now let's get you to the Keeper who'll assign you your duties as a Temple Maiden," Sharriba says instead, "And remember--Do *NOT* tell of our conversation to anyone else here, or outside the Temple. There will be consequences if you do…"

Marrida swallows hard. She doesn't ask what the consequences will be but realises from the Elder's voice it won't be the last time they will remind her of this warning.

They walk to another part of the massive building. Marrida isn't certain if she'd remember the directions in the building; it seems the building's inner structure is endless in its size. She'd never realised how large it really is. The part of it that's visible within Ruh'nar, is a mere fraction of the whole…

Marrida enters a room that Sharriba motions her inside. Here, Marrida is met by sixteen pairs of eyes, all questioning her presence here.

"This is Marrida. Please, Keeper Elydra, can you instruct Marrida also in the duties of a Temple Maiden with the rest of your charges," Sharriba admonishes.

Marrida feels worried all of a sudden when the Elder turns and leaves the room. Marrida looks around, feeling shy. She sees girls and women, all older than she, prodding each other, and there is an undertone of whisper that broke the silence in the room. This far inside the building the sound from the city is absent, she notes.

"Marrida, you can sit over here," Keeper Elydra points at one of the two empty benches to her right. Marrida nods and walks to the place pointed out to her. She sits down, doesn't want to look up for several minutes.

"We were discussing the daily duties before we had Marrida join us," Elder Elydra says, "I'm going to assign everyone in groups of four to work on these duties together…"

Marrida listens as people with unfamiliar names are called out and leave to get on with the initial duties the Elder assigns.

Marrida looks up when her name is called out, and she freezes when a moment later a now very familiar name from earlier in the day, is called out *too*…

CHAPTER FIVE

"So, you think you're good enough to be here…?" the older girl hisses, "Remember my name, little girl, I'm Sarayna, and I'm from a prominent family, unlike you…"

"But my uncle is--" Marrida protests.

"He's *old*. Mark my word. When he's gone, you'll be *out* of here…" Sarayna hisses, though sounding rather threatening.

"No, I won't," Marrida hisses back, "I'm going to be an Acolyte in a year, and--"

Marrida stops speaking, suddenly remembering she's forbidden to say anything about what Elder Sharriba promised her.

"And what…?" Sarayna says.

"Nothing…" Marrida says, and she feels like she's blushing at that moment.

Marrida's attention focuses on what Keeper Elydra is saying. She's going to ignore the continued taunts from the woman next to her, however hard it is. It seems to her, her first day in the Temple is already a day of misery. Deep down, she now regrets the threat she made towards Kalisa about the way she will *be* whenever she gets home.

Kalisa doesn't deserve the treatment she received from me.

She vows to treat her siblings a lot better than the woman beside her seems capable…

Marrida, Sarayna, and three girls, who all seem to know Sarayna and are chatting to her nonstop, all walk towards the large, dark doors of what she already knows as the library. The girls make comments about how the room behind such large doors is either going to be 'scary' or 'dark' or 'dirty'. She chuckles inwardly about the childlike ignorance all four of her companions seem to have.

They enter the room, and the size and number of books there immediately silence them.

She walks towards the first floor of the library; they assigned her to for the duties as a Temple Maiden. She realises she'd rather read books here than do the work. She picks up the small container that holds an ember. From a container, she pours over the oil that will replenish the ember.

Next, Marrida pulls a tinder kit from a small pouch she carries and ignites the ember. Slowly, the flame grows brighter. She watches the flame for a while, letting it mesmerise her. She looks up when she can hear other four girls, also assigned to duties in the library, giggle some distance from her.

For a moment, she wonders what the other girls are giggling about, then she shrugs it off as something that doesn't really concern her. She walks to one table on which numerous books lay. She was told to move any books into their correct place in the library.

In a place as big as this, it will not be a straightforward task, but somehow she feels like this place would be one of the best parts of the Temple. *I wonder if I'll get punished for reading the books.*

She moves her hand over the cover of one book and starts opening it when she hears a sound nearby. She quickly pulls her hand away. She looks around to see if the sound came from so near that she might have been seen. She sees no one.

She moves her hand forward and moves it slowly over the covering of the book. The cover feels soft, almost like it had become this way from many uses.

Marrida sees some writing on the cover, but it was an unfamiliar dialect, *That's not Sab'ruhi.*

Her heart skips a beat when she hears someone giggle in a malicious way near her.

"So, you *like* reading books, I guess…"

Marrida frowns, and when she turns she sees Sarayna, with the three other girls, all standing side by side, and all looking at her in a way she can only describe as disgust or annoyance.

She isn't sure which…

Marrida isn't sure what she can say if she said anything at all. She tries to ignore the woman and girls around her, all laughing at her. She's never experienced anything like this before in her entire life.

Why are they here, and why do they have to be so mean?

She feels tears sting her eyes and does her best not to cry.

"Oooh… look, she's acting like the child she *is*. Maybe she should just go home to Mam and Papa… but then, she hasn't had a Mam and Papa to go to. Just that miserable old uncle of hers…" Sarayna says.

It gets Sarayna, and the girls standing around her, all laughing.

"He's not miserable," Marrida protests.
"Oh, but *he* is. He ended up with a child around him, and one that he *never* wanted…" Sarayna laughs loud. "You don't know what's said about him then. That he's never gone for a life partner because he can't have the *one* he wanted…"

Sarayna laughs again, then she turns and walks away, and the surrounding girls follow too; all of them are laughing as much as she. Marrida stares after them. She has no clue what they're talking about. But, she realises her uncle never spoke much about the family.

One day I'll ask him and insist he tells me.

She now feels angry. And not only at the four females who'd taunted her once more, but deep down also at her uncle for keeping things about her family from her.

Marrida looks at the book again. All of a sudden, she wishes she isn't in the Temple doing any duties as a Temple Maiden. All of a sudden, she doesn't want to be this *Keeper* mentioned by the Elder.

She feels tears well up. She wipes at her eyes when the tears trickle down. She feels so alone all of a sudden…

As the youngest there, it will be almost impossible to make friends with those around her. Some of those who arrived at the Temple are at least a decade older than she…

She sits down at the table and pushes the books aside. She leans her head on her arms and cries. After a while, she looks up and looks around her. There's no sound in the library. She's alone.

"I'll show them. I'll make sure I get as good as the Elder says she'll help me be…" Marrida mutters. She's always told by her uncle she's too stubborn, but now the stubbornness is formulating a plan in her mind.

A plan with consequences, which she won't know about for another five years.

But the plan in her young mind, is to show the surrounding tormentors she's as good, if not better than they…

CHAPTER SIX

Marrida stands on the steps of the Temple for a time, letting the warm sun warm her face. She glances towards the fast disappearing figures of Sarayna and her newly gained friends, now totalling six. Marrida frowns and wonders if she would ever have friends.

But I have friends.

But then she wonders.

Hmm, I wonder who I really have as a friend.

Marrida scowls. She starts her walk home.

Suddenly, she wants to be home, and *be* with the two people, who matter the most to her. Especially after the recent attack from the Wolf Riders, it matters to her. But she knows going home also means she must deal with her duties as a guardian, though in name only, and until she'd done her First Rites; one of them is to dissuade her brother from becoming a soldier in the city. It's a decade before he can be trained at the Academy of Warfare. He can only be accepted after he's been an apprentice of someone for at least three years. Then he told Marrida he'd found a placing to be an apprentice…

Then there's six-year-old Kalisa to deal with. Marrida has to reprimand her for her behaviour, but certainly not in the way she'd suggested in a threat. Now she wants to make up for what happened in the morning, especially after being at the receiving end of taunts herself…

Marrida feels a bit reluctant as she approaches the door of her home. She holds the door handle in her hand for several minutes, standing at her front door to figure out how she's going to make up for the hurtful things she said to her sister that morning. She doesn't know how she's going to explain her change of heart after the way she was treated by someone at the Temple, especially when she can't tell them what she does there.

But she needs to tell her sister how sorry she is for the behaviour of earlier that day.

Marrida opens the door. Inside, the house is silent. Marrida listens, but there are no running footsteps to come and greet her. Not even after she waits for several minutes. It seems she's all alone in the house.

Suddenly a thought occurs to Marrida. They gave her a small package just before leaving the Temple, and the Keeper gave her a stern glance that told her that the package contained something important.

Marrida walks quickly up the stairway and rushes into her sleeping room. She shut her door quietly, then locks it. Locking her sleeping room door is unusual because she doesn't like to leave her siblings out of her life. But today it's different. She needs to see what's in the package, and if it's something from the Temple, they can't know about it…

Marrida reaches in her pocket and pulls the package from it.

She sits down on her bed, and places the package beside her, and looks at it for a moment without knowing what to do next. She feels hesitant about the package. Her fingers caress the cloth in which it's wrapped. She never felt any cloth this soft before. With her finger and thumb Marrida pulls away from the cloth, and then some more, and finally, she moves the last part away. In the cloth, she sees a small pouch and a small folded piece of parchment.

Curious as she is about what's in the pouch, Marrida wants to know what's written on the parchment *first*. She picks it up and unfolds it. It's a letter, and she sees it's written by Elder Sharriba. The letter is about the contents of the pouch.

In the letter, it states the Stone of Truth inside it belonged to Marrida's mother, and she asked Marrida to be given the gem, once she's accepted into the Order of Truth.

She said my mother was Keeper. And this was hers?

Marrida studies the small object carefully. It's like the object the Elder showed, and whereas hers hangs from a silver chain, this object hangs from a gold chain. The colour is as intriguing as it was before when Sharriba showed her own gem to Marrida. Marrida's eyes grow wide at the beauty of the gem, and she realises now the meaning of the Keeper's words.

Marrida turns the gem in her fingers. It's about the size of a rubha apple, the same shade of pale white with a green base, like a part-ripened apple will show during the earliest growing season. Marrida loves those apples, and she smiles when she realises how the gem could easily be mistaken for the apple.

If she hadn't seen the gem beforehand, she might have mistaken the contents of the package for a gift of an apple…

Marrida frowns for a moment, then she wonders why she's given the gem *now*.

From what she gathered from the discussions during the day, only those who'd been in the Temple for few years, two or three or so, are given a gem to use. She's barely a Temple Maiden, and only in an unofficial capacity too, until her First Rites.

I guess I'll have to wait two or three years before I can use this… but…

Marrida speculates in her mind about what her future will be, but her mind is already forming a new, possibly forbidden thought.

I might be able to see my mother's past with this.

She's certain that isn't allowed until she becomes a Keeper, but suddenly the idea seems appealing to her. She listens to make sure she is still alone in the house. It's still completely silent. She wonders again where her brother and sister are, but it doesn't matter.

If they come home and try her sleeping room door, they'll assume she's tired from her day at the Temple and has shut it to allow for her to get sleep. She's curious how the process works with the gem, then recalls what the Elder did. Perhaps the Elder prepared her in some way for this gem, even if she hasn't intended to do this. She feels drawn to the gem and stares intently at it. She's uncertain how to get started, so she searches her mind for the possible clues the Elder gave.

There is something about placing it in one of her hands in a certain way...

CHAPTER SEVEN

Marrida carefully balances the gem on her left hand in the same way as Elder Sharriba had done it. She stares at the gem in her hand and feels stupid suddenly because nothing seems to happen She's certain there's something the Elder had done to make her see the glimpse of her mother.

Marrida closes her eyes to think closer about what had happened while she was in the Elder's chambers.

I'm certain she did something with her hands. She was probably doing it and keeping me occupied with her explanations.

She's certain it is something she can't figure it out.

A door slams shut, which causes Marrida's focus to break from what she's doing. She looks up and hears Kalisa giggle. Esbara says something, followed by more giggles. Marrida frowns, wondering what's so funny for her sister, or for Esbara. Her mind is focused on this gem. She pretends to be asleep if either of them knocks on her sleeping room door.

Marrida waits for several minutes, wondering if soon there will be a knock on her door, but no one turns up.

She shrugs her shoulders and turns her attention back to the gem. She moves it from her right hand to her left. She feels a warm sensation. She's about to pick up the gem when she feels the same earlier disorienting energy surge through her body.

And then, there is darkness…

The energy's effect grips her mind. She panics. She feels like she's sinking into the deepest part of a lake. Then the whispers come. Marrida isn't sure where they come from. She tries to look around, but she sees only the darkness.

After a few moments, the whispers become louder. She wonders who's talking.

Are they talking to me, or am I hearing someone else? What's going on?

She sees a woman, then smiles when she realises who it is. It's her mother, but a much younger version of her. A moment later the image is gone. It replaces itself with the image of an old woman who smiles an enigmatic smile.

Is that my grandmother?

She looks at the old woman, who seems to have silver-grey hair, soft lines on her face, and who seems ageless.

But no answer comes from the woman or her own mind. Marrida never knew her grandmother. She knows nothing about her mother's or father's parents. She knows from her uncle they died a few years before her birthing. Her mother was from Marridina, and she never spoke of her parents or whether she had any siblings…

Marrida is uncertain how long this strange experience will last when it's over, or long afterwards, Marrida lifts herself up from the bed.

Was that a vision?

She reaches up to her head, which seems painful for unknown reasons. She reaches for a cup and the pitcher of water she always has beside her bed, and pours in water, and drinks almost all of it. She pours more of the water into her cup and sits thinking about what she experienced while sipping from the water. One thing clear from the vision is that she needs a lot of practice to do it right and to see anything from it that makes sense.

Marrida can work out she saw her mother and can only assume that the other person she saw was her maternal grandmother. She doesn't know if she can see the past of other people. Her mind concludes it to be her grandmother, and for almost another half decade that's the view, she'll maintain until other events give her a new perspective of this vision.

The vision leaves Marrida feeling like she is close to discovering something of her own past; this isn't it going to be easy while she still has to learn every part of this thing called *Keeper*.

She doesn't even understand what the term means.

Like everyone else, she knows of the Order of Truth only as something mystical, something is spoken of as a rumour, but now she is a part of it.

But I was told not to tell about it. Is it that bad if people outside it know about it…?

She remembers both the Elder's and Keeper's tone when they each warned the girl about consequences if she spoke about what goes on inside the Order of Truth.

"I wonder what would happen if I *tell* someone. For example, if I told my brother and sister," Marrida wonders. "Should I tell them…?"

Renewed laughter from downstairs takes Marrida's mind away from the thought pattern that is settling in her mind.

Maybe I tell them much later when I know I can get them to keep the secret safe. They're too young to be burdened with that right now.

She gets up, straightens her clothing, and looks in her mirror, and she tries to make a face that says, *"You just woke me up from the noise…"*

Marrida unlocks her door quietly, then opens the door, and walks out of her room to the stairway, and descends it and enters the front room, from where the quiet voices of her siblings had drifted towards her.

The moment she enters the room, Kalisa rushes at Marrida with an embrace. "We didn't want to wake you…" she says, "… are you hungry from your work at the Temple? I made soup…"

Marrida nods.

Marrida sits down on the chair she usually sat in, close to the fireplace. She glances at Esbara and sees him studying her.

Although Kalisa has the innocence of a child still, he doesn't, and he's getting more and more inquisitive about the world around them. She sees him frown, like he wants to say something, but stops himself from saying it. Marrida wonders about what is on his mind.

Before they can speak about whatever they're thinking, Kalisa walks into the front room announcing she has the soup heating up, and they'll eat in an hour. This distracts Marrida and Esbara, who both instead spend time entertaining their younger sibling with stories and games. Kalisa doesn't notice the increased uncaring feelings developing between her siblings.

They'd need to continue their discussion about Esbara's future. Esbara also feels that Marrida has been overly unkind earlier in that day towards Kalisa, and he is protective of his younger sibling, even in regards to Marrida. Esbara also notices something different about Marrida now. She promised to tell them about the Temple, and so far she hasn't done any of that…

The evening is quiet, somewhat subdued. Marrida has trouble following the discussion going on between Esbara and Kalisa. They're talking about their visit to Uncle Joharan, and something about a new apprentice who has just arrived. And they talk also about a journey to a lake their uncle has planned during summer…

CHAPTER EIGHT

Marrida walks through the silent streets. She'd decided today to go as early as possible to the Temple, and therefore also to avoid any confrontation with Sarayna, who'd made it a point to wait for her at the exit of the long street where Marrida lives. Marrida feels nervous as she enters the massive square. It's devoid of even the earliest visiting merchants, who'd gather there at the northern side of the square, opposite of the massive Temple.

She listens for what might be the voices of others going to the Temple, but she's there before them. When she sees the massive doors of the Temple open, she rushes towards them. The Keeper opening the heavy doors gives a surprised glance as Marrida rushes past her into the Temple without even waiting to see if she's permitted to go inside.

After checking to make sure there's definitely no other Temple Maiden or any of the Acolytes there, Marrida rushes through the vestibule, up the stairway, and is in the silence of the massive library only minutes later. It will become a routine for her for almost the next five years…

Marrida looks around. She isn't sure if she's allowed to look at any books, so after a few minutes of indecision, she walks to one of the five massive windows and looks outside. She looks at the massive garden of the Temple, and realises she can hardly see the other end of it, she wonders how large the building really is.

I should go look around the garden when I have time.

Marrida isn't certain if she's allowed to do that. She sits staring from the window and therefore doesn't realise that Elder Sharriba has quietly sat herself down next to her. She jerks from her dreamy pondering when the Elder coughs gently, mostly to let the girl know she isn't alone.

When Sharriba sees she has Marrida's attention, she smiles gently at the girl then says, "I hope you didn't feel too out-of-place yesterday…"

Marrida shakes her head, feeling somewhat tongue-tied. She rarely feels this shy. She smiles back at the Elder before she speaks, "I hope it's alright for me to be here in the library…" she whispers.

"Of course," Sharriba says, "You'll spend a lot of time here with *me*. You have *much* to learn…"

"The Keeper gave me a gem yesterday…"

She reaches in her pocket and pulls the small gem from it.

"That was your mother's gem. You'll use it now," Sharriba says, "It passes on from mother to daughter. Wear around your neck, but keep it hidden from view at all times. Only those, who are in the Order, may know of its existence."

Marrida nods, then she asks, "When will I learn about using it?"

Sharriba notices the hesitation in the girl's voice as she speaks.

"I want you to be proficient as fast as possible. I got my… reasons that you have to do this…"

It is Marrida's turn to notice hesitation.

She looks down, nodding to acknowledge she understands, but by looking down she's able to avoid having the Elder notice that she has noticed the Elder's hesitation.

"How long will it take to learn?"

"It will take *many* years, it depends on how proficient you are," Sharriba says, "Some learn it faster than others. Some *never* learn at all. There's a few in the group who came with you who are like that…"

Marrida frowns, then nods.

She doesn't feel it's her place to ask whom the Elder might be referring to, but it already appears that the 'some' doesn't include her. At least, she hopes that's the case.

"Come with me…" Sharriba says.

For the second day in a row, Marrida follows the enigmatic leader of the Temple. This time their destination isn't the Elder's chambers, but a part of the Temple Marrida hadn't even realised, exists.

Sharriba opens a door. The warm breeze on Marrida's face explains the destination of this trek through the Temple. Her eyes fly open when she sees the exquisite gardens she only glimpsed before from a window in the library. She grins at the Elder.

"The Temple is much larger than you realise," Sharriba says softly, "But this building dwarfs next to the earliest buildings marking the beginning of our Order…"

"How old is the Order?"

"The earliest days are some three thousand years, or more, in the past, and it's a past Keeper, even the best of them, have *no* access to in visions. Therefore, we've to rely on what's written in the many books in this library, and some of them are as old as the Order itself. There are some books, rumoured to be older…"

"So the Order is three thousand years old, and why can't we see that far back?"

"We don't know. It's something I'm concerned about for many reasons, and--" Sharriba starts to say, but she stops in mid-sentence, short of explaining those reasons.

Marrida notices the sadness in the woman's voice as she speaks. She notes the hesitation in what the woman says, or *not* says, almost like the Elder wants to say more, but something stops her.

A little while later, Sharriba motions for Marrida to follow her. Marrida follows Sharriba as they walk to some benches in the sunnier part of the massive garden. They sit down, and Marrida looks up at the Elder expectantly and waits for the Elder to continue her explanation.

"There are *many* things you don't know yet, and I don't know when I'm able to tell you about it," Sharriba continues, "But one day, it will *be* important for you to be skilled as with the skills I'm going to teach you. Although you're actually *too* young to learn, there are reasons at play why you need to learn them faster…"

Marrida nods, then she feels surprised when the Elder winks at her.

"I'm supposed to keep to the rules myself, but if we *do* this whenever we're alone, and if you don't mention it, then no one else will know it," Elder Sharriba explains, "I can tell you the reason for us *not* being able to see so far into the past, is tied to the things that happened in the Order in the last thousand years. Some of those reasons, you'll learn about in your normal lessons, but there's other information that one day you'll have to ask about from *someone* specific…"

Sharriba stops speaking, and after a while, it's clear to Marrida she isn't going to get the answer as to who the 'someone' is in the Elder's explanation moments earlier…

CHAPTER NINE

Marrida pauses in her task when she hears voices approaching. She looks up and feels disappointment when she sees it's Sarayna accompanied by five girls, and they're all walking in her direction.

"Ah, so you're still here…" Sarayna says coldly, "But, I guess the Elder needs someone as *her* entertainment because I guess she gets so lonely in this place…"

"What do you want?" Marrida does not try to hide how annoyed and angry she feels.

"It doesn't matter what I want. You want to be *gone* from here. You don't belong in this place, *little* child…" Sarayna says.

"I was selected to be here. I'm going to learn to be a Keeper," Marrida feels increasingly angrier.

"Oh, really. I'd like to see *you* get skill the size of a rubha gem-sized. I bet you'll be past Second Rites *before* you even get your first vision…" Sarayna says coldly.

Marrida frowns but doesn't answer.

She can't tell this woman that she's already used a Stone of Truth, and she's certain Sarayna will use the knowledge against her.

"So, now you lost the ability to speak. Good. It means *your* whiny voice won't disturb me while I do my important tasks." Sarayna turns and walks to the other end of the room with her entourage in tow.

Marrida returns to her task; a task given to her by the Elder. After giving the girl her first lesson in the more ancient parts of the history of the Order, which according to the Elder is normally only taught after *three* years as an Acolyte, she told the girl to prepare batches of parchment for transcribing some older texts onto fresh parchment.

First Marrida pours oil, which to her smells like an oil her uncle uses for his work, onto a square-shaped stone slab. Only a few drops are needed, and this oil is used to give the parchment its suppleness. She uses a brush to spread the oil around, then places one of the untreated parchments on top. With the brush, which is now coated with some oil, she brushes over the parchment. After that, she pours a grey, fine ash over it. The ash will react with the oils and allow the parchment to become supple after a few hours of soaking. The next part after this will require each parchment to be scrubbed and then washed.

After one further treatment with the oil, they will be left to dry completely in the sun until three days have passed. Then the parchments are ready for use. The treatment doesn't just make them supple, but the scrubbing causes them to stretch to the thin consistency of good parchment.

Marrida glances occasionally in the direction of Sarayna, and the surrounding girls, mostly whenever she hears them giggle.

She wonders what they are talking about, and why she isn't invited in for a chat. But she knows why.

Sarayna seems to have a deep dislike for her, and Marrida isn't even sure why the woman dislikes her. She is probably five or six younger, but that isn't a reason to behave in that way.

It is the first time in Marrida's life that she has encountered this sort of behaviour, and she doesn't know how she will cope with it for the next decade or more…

"You're doing it all wrong…" Sarayna calls out.

"No, I'm doing it the way I was told to do it by…" Marrida begins saying.

"Of course, you're doing it wrong. You're doing it like a *child*," Sarayna laughs menacingly, it causes chills to go up Marrida's spine.

Marrida isn't certain why Sarayna seems to dislike her, but it's clear she does everything she can to single out the girl.

The experience, if she can call it that, is new to Marrida, and no one has ever prepared her for it. She wonders if she can talk to Elder Sharriba about it, but is uncertain if her new mentor will believe her.

After completing her task, and making sure the cabinet with the parchments being treated is locked, Marrida walks out of the room, and doesn't even glance in the direction of the other girls, and the few women, also there. She made sure to lock the cabinet because she doesn't want to come back to Sarayna's possible sabotage of her task.

Marrida knocks on the door at the end of the corridor and quickly glances over her shoulder to make sure she is alone, or that her new tormentors followed her here.

The corridor behind her is empty. "Come in…" a muffled voice calls out from within the room behind the door.

Marrida opens the door and finds herself in a small room with two Keepers sitting on either end of a table. There are two benches on either side, both empty.

"I believe you're the girl the Elder sent to us for an afternoon of lessons. My name is Keeper Cheryssa. This here is Keeper Elythia," Cheryssa says.

Marrida sits down, and she waits for what is going to happen next.

"We're teaching you the skills to do a vision. It's a skill not easily mastered, and few become very strong in the skill," Elythia explains.

"You have the gem the Elder wanted you to have with you?" Cheryssa asks.

Marrida nods and pulls the gem up from under her tunic. She placed the necklace with the gem on it around her neck, like the Elder suggested she should do. She looks down at the gem hanging from the golden chain for a moment, before placing the gem on the table in front of her.

"Do you know anything about the history of these gems?" Cheryssa asks.

"Only what Elder Sharriba told me about it yesterday. The gem was my mother's gem, and Keepers have used it for three thousand years to look at the past," Marrida replies.

"It's not as simple as that. But the information is a start," Elythia says, "There are *many* gaps in our knowledge of the history, unfortunate as that may be, but we're most certain of the events of the last fifteen hundred years."

"How long has the current version of the Order existed then?" Marrida asks.

"Yes, the Order as it exists now was established between fifteen hundred and a thousand years ago. Fifteen hundred years ago, the First Elder wrote down the methods of learning the skill as we're about to teach you," Elythia replies.

"And I'm going to learn all that?" Marrida asks.

"Some of it you'll learn *today*. The parts that relate to the use of the gem," Cheryssa says.

Marrida smiles, but she feels nervous now. She hopes these two women won't notice she already has experimented with the gem. She knows from the previous day's comment that it's probably not only dangerous for her but also forbidden…

CHAPTER TEN

Cheryssa nods at Marrida. She has had her practice the method of holding the gem for the last hour. She wonders for a moment why she has to do the same actions over and over, and it's starting to irritate her deep down. But every time the Keeper says: *"Again"*

Marrida does as instructed and picks the gem back up from the table with her right hand.

She stretches her left hand out in front of her chest and places the gem on her flat-stretched fingers, and wills it to stay there in a balanced way.

"That's perfect..."

Marrida smiles at Cheryssa and is greeted with a warm smile back.

"As long as you remember the rule that you cannot do visions by yourself, you can do this exercise at home every day," Cheryssa says, "I understand you have a brother and sister. They cannot know about this exercise or another part of what you learn here, understood?"

Marrida nods.

"Now, I want you to close your eyes after you've done the exercise to hold the gem in the correct way. When you do that, keep your eyes closed until I speak again," Elythia says.

Marrida picks the gem up from the table in the way she was instructed before, then after she's certain the gem is on her hand in the correct way, she closes her eyes and waits.

She waits. It's an unknown period later when she senses

something near her…

Marrida feels the urge to open her eyes, but remembers that she has to keep them shut as instructed by the Keeper.

"Marrida… Marrida…"

Marrida feels herself involuntarily frown. "Whose voice is that?" she wonders, "That's neither of the Keepers…"

She decides to listen to the voice. It has a melodic quality to it, and whoever it belongs to, is someone older for certain.

Could it be my grandmother whom I sensed in the vision before…?

"Marrida…"

Now the voice is the more familiar one of Cheryssa, and a moment later Marrida senses a hand on her shoulder. She opens her eyes and is surprised to find both Keepers standing by her side, and both look concerned.

"What happened?" Marrida is surprised that her voice sounds like she has some sort of coughing sickness.

"Drink this," Elythia says gently. Marrida takes the cup being held out to her, and drinks from the cool water in it. After several sips, she places the cup on the table. She looks from side to side to the Keepers, who have each sat down on the bench beside her, enveloping her with their presences.

"What happened?" she asks again.

The Keepers look at one another before Cheryssa answers, "We think you did your first vision without even realising it."

"I did… a vision…?" Marrida feels shocked and hopes it doesn't mean they've discovered her indiscretion of the previous day.

"There are *few* who are this strong in their skill. Perhaps, you don't remember, but I was one of those who came with Elder Sharriba when she came to find you," Elythia says, "I was uncertain at the time why she'd have interest in you. There are… certain things she'll tell you eventually if she can. Those things, she'll tell you, are the things that mustn't go beyond the few who know it. She knows, we also know because she trusts us, but most here do not know… and none of the Acolytes or other Temple Maiden can know…"

"Know what?" Marrida asks hesitantly.

"It's perhaps *too* early for you to know. It's best you put this all out of your mind for the next few years and instead concentrate on everything you else you will also learn while you're here…" Cheryssa states.

Marrida nods but feels unsure whether this is some warning to let her know they know about her indiscretion, or that it's a genuine indicator of her potential skill. She feels vulnerable since the first moment when she'd arrived, and this conversation doesn't make her feel any more secure.

They spend the remainder of the afternoon talking about the history of the gem. Marrida asked questions, but her mind is in turmoil. She can't get out of her mind that the Keepers stated she *did* a vision.

Why did she of all people have the ability to do these visions so fast? What was so significant about what the Keepers said about being strong in this skill?

The two Keepers have their own thoughts about what has happened that they decided not to voice in front of the girl.

But right now, her lessons are more important than what their opinion might be. They'd go to the Elder and discuss with her the details of what has happened, and then she could decide on the next steps to take.

"The First Elder came from the east. We're uncertain where from, but it's said that she, and two others, are those who established the Order as it exists now. It existed before, but not as structured as it's now," Cheryssa says.

"How long has this Temple existed?" Marrida asks.

"We don't know exactly, but it was before the First Elder. It's at least a thousand years old," Elythia says, "It has a mysterious past, and no one, not even Elder Sharriba, knows what that past is… No one knows about that ancient past…"

"Some say there are books hidden away in places that most cannot reach or want to reach. Elder Sharriba has often said that she wants to find those books, but there's no way to know where to even start looking for them," Cheryssa says.

"Are those books as old as some books in the library?" Marrida asks.

"No, some are much older," Cheryssa smiles. Cheryssa notices how the interest of this girl is far greater than most others who have recently joined the Order.

"Why does Elder Sharriba want them?" Marrida flinches for a moment because she's certain she's asked something she couldn't know about yet, but is surprised when she gets a reply to her question.

"There's a city far to the northeast, which is one of the earliest places for the Order to exist. However, the city has been cut off from outside influences for a thousand years. In that city, they say it is also the only place where the northern invaders were present until very recent. That city, and one other," Cheryssa says.

"We have no answer why we cannot see the past of that far back, and there's so much missing information, that it means we rely heavily on the visions we do," Elythia says.

Marrida is surprised at the frankness of the two women. She remembers the words and vows that she'll help…

CHAPTER ELEVEN

Marrida climbs the stairway inside the tower. She often stared at the tower from the square, long before she knew that one day she'd be walking inside the walls of the Temple. It seems the stairs want to keep winding upwards. She stops for a moment and tries to peer from a small window in the wall, but whoever built the tower, they did it intending to make it impossible for a young girl like Marrida to glance out…

Marrida is surprised by the size of the room at the top of the tower. The tower seems too slender to house a room of this size. It seems old and seems also like no has used it in many years, or even decades. Marrida looks around. Although the tower itself is round, the room is shaped like a hexagon. Each wall of the hexagon has two large fading portraits on them, each facing one another.

Marrida isn't able to determine who or what the portraits represent and pulls her nose up when her finger entangles itself with the fine cobweb that seems to cover the portraits.

I wonder who these people are?

She looks closer at the portraits, and notices they seem older than reality dictated. "This room is part of that old past that the Keepers mentioned to you…"

Marrida spins around. Elder Sharriba stands at the doorway, and unlike her, it seems she isn't breathless from a climb up to the top of the spire. Marrida is uncertain how the Elder knows she came to this room.

"I should go. I didn't know I wasn't supposed to come here," Marrida walks towards the stairs. But as she approaches the doorway, Sharriba's hand stops her.

"I think you have a *right* to know what's going on," she says softly, "Sit down, and I'll tell you what I can about *this* room. Not all of it, because you'll learn more later. But enough, so you understand your place here…"

Marrida sits down on a small stool, and Sharriba sits down on a bench near the window.

"It's a room of sorrow, Marrida, because in this room they changed the fate of many," Sharriba begins, "It's also here where I was told they selected me to be the next Elder…"

"Was it bad to be chosen?" Marrida asks hesitantly.

"There were reasons why it was bad, but I cannot tell those right now. One day, you'll be explained why, and then you must promise yourself to use that knowledge with care," Sharriba says.

"I promise…"

"This room was used by the previous Elder, and it was used by all those who came before *her*," Sharriba says, "There's a reason *why* I don't use it. It's linked with *that* history filled with sorrow. I don't want to be reminded of it every day…"

"I always wondered what this tower was for, that's why I climbed here…"

"Curiosity can be a good thing, but be careful with it. In the wrong place, and the wrong time, it can cause more harm than good," Sharriba says.

Marrida nods.

"The history of this Temple dates back about seventeen hundred years. Another building stood in what's now the garden," Sharriba says, "It burnt down in mysterious circumstances according to the texts, then about a hundred years later, the new building… this one… was built in its place…"

"Does anyone know why the other building burned down?"

"Some say it was the northern invaders who came and attacked this city…" Sharriba says.

"I thought they left a long time before that…"

"It's believed that some of them stayed around and that there are still some around now…" Sharriba says.

Marrida sits silently, looking around the room for a while. She looks at each fading portrait, and again wonders who the women in them are. In particular, she's intrigued by the old woman in the portrait behind the Elder.

"Who is she?" she asks impulsively.

Sharriba turns to look at the portrait the girl is pointing at. "That's the First Elder. The one you were taught about earlier…" Sharriba smiles at the girl.

"She is pretty…"

"You think so?" Sharriba asks.

"Yes, she has beautiful green eyes. Actually, they're like your," Marrida says, feeling shy suddenly.

"My mother always told me my eyes, are the colour of rubha apples," Sharriba replies, "And I believe your mother always said your eyes are the colour of a bright summer sky…"

Marrida smiles. She remembered her mother telling that often.

"I miss my mother," Marrida says.

"I'm certain you do," Sharriba replies, "But as your co-guardian, you *can* regard me as a surrogate mother. I'd like that…"

"I would like that too," Marrida smiles at the Elder. Marrida suddenly feels a lot happier than she's felt in days. It seems that the Elder is showing her she has a friend here in the Temple.

Neither of them really realises that this beginning of an unusual friendship will have more consequences than either knows at that moment…

They talk a while longer, with the Elder explaining more about who each in the portrait represented. Marrida discovers that the six women shown were the first six Elders of the Temple. Marrida sits listening wide-eyed to the Elder as she explains the details about the Temple she's only guessed at up to now.

When it's time for Marrida to go home, she's pensive about what she learnt about the past. She strolls towards home and isn't even aware that the next day life will start changing for her.

As she enters the house, Marrida looks over her shoulders at the street. She senses something but isn't sure what. She looks in both directions. She doesn't realise the skills she's taught that day give her heightened sense of awareness of her surroundings.

Marrida walks into her house and is greeted by Kalisa's rush to greet and hug her.

"Esbara said he wanted to go out…" Kalisa says.

"Go out where?" Marrida asks.

"He said many city guardsmen are gathering at the eastern gate for some reason. So, he went to look at them…"

"You mean to say he's out now?" Marrida feels angry at her brother for leaving Kalisa alone.

Kalisa nods.

"Put on your cloak. We'll go get him…" Marrida says.

Kalisa got her cloak, and a few minutes later the two girls are walking to the eastern gate. When they get there, they find the gatehouse in turmoil.

"They're coming… sound the alarm…" a voice calls out.

Marrida ignores the warning for a moment, although her mind

instinctively knows what the alarm is for.

She grabs Esbara by the wrist and drags him with her... back home.

CHAPTER TWELVE

When they're home again, Marrida shouts at Esbara, "You know what that alarm means…"

"I know, but I was being careful…" Esbara shouts back.

"They're coming, and you were in the street. If they grab you…" Marrida says.

They both stop talking when they notice Kalisa's sobbing. Marrida and Esbara both kneel next to the girl. "Why do you need to argue so much…" Kalisa says, and she gulps a few sobs.

"We don't mean to…" Marrida says.

She stares hard at Esbara opposite of her. He looks at her for a moment, then looks at his younger sister.

"We don't mean to…" he says, echoing Marrida's words.

They all walk into the front room, sit down, but are all silent for a while, uncertain what to say. Marrida and Esbara stare at one another across the room. All the happy feeling of going home to talk with her siblings has left Marrida. She's angry about the suggestion her brother made.

"You know it's unsafe for boys whenever they come," she says, "They'll snatch you, and if that happens we'll never see you again. None who get snatched ever makes it home again…"

"I was going to be careful…" Esbara says.

"I know you're careful, but this isn't like the tunnels. These are dangerous men. Out to make life worse for us in the city," Marrida says softly.

"I know that. But one day, I'll sort them out. I'm going to be a soldier to defend the city," Esbara says.

"That's a dangerous thing too," Marrida replies, "I forbid it…"

"When I've done my Second Rites, you can't dictate what I do. When I've done First Rites I become Kalisa's co-guardian, and you can't order a co-guardian around," Esbara retorts.

"Until then, I'm the one who decides," Marrida says.

An hour later, after much talking, Kalisa announces she's sorting out the evening meal. She walks off and lets out a sigh when she hears her two siblings start again with their argument in the front room. She busies herself with cooking a meal of vegetables and some leftover meat from the previous day. Usually, the task makes the young girl feel happy, but she isn't happy tonight. Something bothers her about the argument between her siblings, and Kalisa can't figure out what it is. She feels something has changed ever since her sister went to the Temple…

Kalisa walks into the front room somewhat hesitantly, and says, "Evening meal is ready…"

Silently Marrida and Esbara get up, and they walk single file into the kitchen, followed a few moments later by Kalisa. They sit down at the kitchen table. They all look at one another for a moment, then Kalisa speaks, "Can we talk about fun stuff instead of all the boring things you two talk about…?"

Marrida and Esbara look at one another, then they nod silently.

"Esbara, are you going to tell Marrida about the new apprentice Uncle Joharan has recruited?" Kalisa smiles broadly now.

"What new apprentice?"

"It's a boy called Damir," Esbara says. "Uncle Joharan says, he met him while he was walking near the old tunnels…"

"Oh… him…" Marrida says. "He was there when I visited two

weeks ago. But I didn't know why he was there…"

"Apparently Uncle Joharan asked for him…" Kalisa says. "He's nice…"

"Ah, so you like him already?" Marrida says teasingly.

She giggles when Kalisa turns bright red. "Ermm… yes…" Kalisa says, looking down shy now.

"So, what sort of person is he then?" Esbara asks, now joining in with Marrida to tease their younger sister.

"He's nice…" Kalisa says.

Marrida smiles. She knows Kalisa has few friends, so a new friend, and one that her uncle trusts, is a good thing. Esbara and Marrida look at each other, then both laugh loud.

"I guess you wanted us to stop arguing," Marrida says, "I think you succeeded…"

Kalisa beams a smile at each of her siblings.

"So what is it he does there?" Marrida asks.

"Apparently, he's going to learn from Uncle Joharan to be an artisan," Kalisa says.

"I've met him too. Apparently, he's from the eastern quarter of the city. He has brothers and sisters, and his parents aren't well off," Esbara says.

"Uncle says he's going to give Damir a pack with food and other stuff every week for him to bring home to his family," Kalisa says.

"Sounds good," Marrida says. "Perhaps, you should bring him here for a visit next week. So I can meet him too…"

"I'll ask him…" Kalisa says, "Oh, I have to show you what he made for me today…"

Before Marrida can say anything Kalisa gets up and runs to the front room. They wait silently for Kalisa to return. After several minutes of waiting, both older siblings frown and wonder why Kalisa is taking so long. Marrida looks at Esbara.

"Is she ever going to come back in the room? She still has her food to finish," Marrida says.

"I think she went upstairs," Esbara says.

"But she said it was in the front room," Marrida says.

"I think she remembered she took it to her room," Esbara replies.

"She's probably doing it on purpose," Marrida says, "You know how she is…"

"True," Esbara replies, "I guess we have us a future city leader here…"

Marrida laughs.

"I guess so," she says.

"Ahh, so now the two of you can be civil." Kalisa glances around the doorway, grinning at her siblings, who both give her an annoyed stare. Their stares make Kalisa grin more.

"I think I'll grab the thing Damir made now," she says, and before either of her siblings can say anything, she's gone again.

A few minutes later she comes back carrying a wooden object. As she approaches the table, Esbara helps her hoist it onto the table. Marrida looks at it.

"What is that?" Marrida asks.

"It's a carving of horses like they existed hundreds and hundreds of years ago," Kalisa says.

"How does he know about them?" Marrida asks.

"I described the painting in the front room to him. He carved these based on my description of them," Kalisa says.

"He's good…" Marrida says.

"Yes, he is good…" Esbara says.

"Maybe get him to draw something to show us that he brings with him…" Marrida suggests.

"I can do that…" Kalisa says, "What would you want him to draw…?"

"Something special to him…" Marrida smiles now.

"I'll talk to him tomorrow…" Kalisa says.

"Good. But now, finish your meal…" Marrida says.

CHAPTER THIRTEEN

Marrida sighs when she sees her new day will start badly, seeing that Sarayna and her entourage waiting on the pavement, just outside the Temple. Marrida still can't get herself to call them some friends to the woman.

"Ah, so you've still not given up here then…" Sarayna says sarcastically when she sees Marrida.

"Why don't you leave me alone?" Marrida asks.

"Because, little *girl*, you don't belong in this place…" Sarayna says.

"Elder Sharriba says I *do*, and--" Marrida says, but she stops when she realises she's about to reveal the lessons with the Elder to make her more skilled.

"And…?" Sarayna says, but she sounds patronising and almost obnoxious when she asks.

Marrida stays silent. She sighs. Over the heads of the girls, she looks at the door of the Temple to see if it's open yet. Marrida feels happier when she finally sees the doors of the Temple open. Her tormentors stop the moment they hear the doors opening… behind them.

They grin, then turn and walk off into the Temple like nothing has been going on. After a moment of hesitation, Marrida follows them inside.

Inside, Elder Sharriba stands waiting for the group of girls together with six Keepers, some of whom Marrida recognised while most are unknown to her. Sharriba raises an eyebrow when she sees how Marrida evades every attempt from her to return her smile. She looks at the other girls and realises something has happened moments before that makes Marrida nervous.

She seems nervous…

Elder Sharriba knows the reason, perhaps, that causes Marrida to behave so erratic. She whispers to the Keeper beside her, then turns and walks off.

"Elder Sharriba has stated that today we're to practise Stone Bonding. She says we need to place two opposites together, and any attempt to cause discord during the exercise *will* be punished severely," Rudrina says.

Marrida doesn't realise that by avoiding to look at the Elder, she also missed the introduction of the four Keepers here whom she didn't yet know.

"There are forty-eight of you who will do this training. We're going to make four groups from you, then each group gets paired up in twos," Rudrina continues explaining.

Marrida smiles inwardly when she sees that Sarayna and her entourage end up being split up among the four groups with Sarayna on her own in the group being led by Cheryssa. Marrida looks up at Cheryssa and smiles at the woman. Cheryssa gives a slight nod, smiles ever so briefly, then looks stern again.

She's instructed to make Marrida feel secure, but also needs to teach the girl a valuable lesson. The words of the Elder have Cheryssa wondering about the girl's future.

"She's destined for something other than here. She's foretold…"

Cheryssa has supported the Elder in her efforts to undo the harm done within the walls of the Temple in ages long gone by. She can't quite grasp what the harm may have been; she's able to guess some of it from the texts in the books she's read over the last twenty years she's been at the Temple.

The twelve girls assigned to Cheryssa, which includes Marrida, all followed the Keeper to a room on the ground floor and a short distance from the Temple's massive entry doors. These doors are now being closed by some other Keepers with the help of some Temple Maidens.

Marrida feels concern grow as the vestibule becomes darker, although it never is totally dark unless it is nighttime. Some well-positioned windows spread a soft bluish light. It's a shade of colour which reminds her of her mother's light blue eyes.

Inside the room, they line the girls up in two rows opposite of one another. Marrida thinks the girl opposite of her will be the one to be paired up with her for whatever Keeper Cheryssa has in mind… or more precisely, whatever it is the Elder wants Cheryssa to do. Marrida waits as anxiously as the rest of the girls.

"The task that's before you, is to attune yourself to your Stone of Truth. Please take the gem from its necklace and hold it in your left hand," Cheryssa says, "I'm now going to pair you up, however for this to be done in the fairest way, all of you need to be blindfolded beforehand…."

Marrida doesn't know when another Keeper came into the room, but a moment later she feels a soft cloth cover over her eyes. The sounds from the other girls show they too feel surprised by the sudden action. When Marrida tries to reach up to the blindfold, someone pushes her hands down, and rather forcefully too. A moment later a voice softly whispers.

"It's all a way to teach those who think they're the strongest because they can bully people a hard lesson in humility… I've got it all planned out, and you'll be stronger from it too…"

Marrida smiles when she realises that one of those assisting, is the Elder herself. She isn't sure how long the Elder will stay, however. She wonders what lesson is going to be learnt really today. She waits for the lesson. She nervously holds the gem in her left hand.

"Please raise your left hand up, with the gem in the centre of the palm…" Cheryssa says.

Marrida does as instructed, and finds the task more difficult than she imagined with the blindfold over her eyes. But she wants to succeed more than before now, because of what the Elder whispered to her. She doesn't want to fail this task. If she succeeded, and those, who thought they're strong by looking down on others failed, she will walk away from this all strong and more self-assured than she'd been in weeks. Marrida starts to feel the familiar warmth, and then hears the surprised gasps and also a few that sound afraid, she realises what the Elder did a few days earlier.

Now it becomes clear the Elder has something more than just extra lessons in mind. It will show to the other girls that one who's so much younger than them also can do the exercises in equal measure.

Most, but not all, will become accepting of the girl, which in turn would make her life much more tolerable...

The glow in Marrida's hand intensified gradually. Someone can easily have placed an ember into the palm of her hand, and Marrida would have believed that person. Even though, Marrida feels more assured because of the Elder's words, after a time, even she gets so much discomfort from the exercise that she feels the temptation to take the gem from her hand, and hold it in her other hand.

Marrida grasps her skirt with her right hand to resist the urge to grab the stone. Then the feeling replaces itself with another...

CHAPTER FOURTEEN

Marrida feels a wave of surprise wash over her when this other feeling comes. There's no feeling ever she experienced before that equals what she feels right now. The heat in her hand has gone away, and now she senses the sensation of people whispering around her. Marrida listens.

First, Marrida thinks that those around her in the room are whispering, but she can also hear men's voices whisper. She knows they're forbidden to enter the Temple, and what she can see of the building makes it clear that what she sees isn't anything in this Temple.

Also, these voices aren't any she recognises as belonging to her mother, or any other person she knows. A wave of confusion hits her then. Despite it, she tries to listen to what these unknown people are saying. The voices sound strange to Marrida's ears. It isn't the Sab'ruhi dialect. She is uncertain what dialect it is. But as she can't see anything, it's hard for her to determine their appearances.

If only my eyes weren't blindfolded…

She feels her right hand reach up, and Marrida frowns because there is no blindfold there. She opens her eyes and is surprised to see her surroundings.

Where am I…? It is not Ruh'nar.

That's something Marrida is certain of. But where she is, and also why she's there, those are two questions she isn't able to answer.

I must speak to Elder Sharriba about this…

She tries to change the setting, however much she tries she can't do it. It's getting her frustrated. She also can't move. The whispers are now becoming louder. They're voices speaking instead now, and if only she can understand the dialect spoken, it will tell her more of what's going on. Both wherever she is, and whatever is going on with her. Then, one voice seems to come from her left. With extreme effort, she turns to see who speaks, and she sees two men standing there, who seemed to talk to a woman. The image of them is there for only a few seconds before it disappears and blackness fills the space around Marrida once more. It also becomes silent.

No whispers or louder voices can be heard anywhere around Marrida. Then a single voice speaks. Still not any voice she recognises, but now she can at least try to concentrate on that voice alone. It's a woman's voice, perhaps older, but not as old as the voice of Elder Sharriba. It isn't any of the Keepers she has met so far.

Something about the voice intrigues Marrida, and she feels herself smile. She feels like she knows something the other people around her, don't know, or can't know.

"Remember this…" the voice says.

Marrida frowns. She wonders who it is the voice spoke the words to because she is sure it isn't to her.

"It is crucial you remember this for when you visit the city that's built against the spires…" the voice says.

Marrida feels confused. It's almost like they give a message to her, but why…

The darkness comes back, and this time doesn't feel comfortable anymore. Instead, it makes Marrida feel like she wants this, whatever this is, to end and end soon. She becomes aware of someone shaking her shoulder gently, and once more, and then again with added urgency.

"Marrida… Marrida…"

Marrida frowns again. This time the voice is familiar. She thinks it's Keeper Cheryssa who said her name.

"Huh… what?" she says. Her throat feels dry, and she wonders why her voice sounds so odd.

"Marrida, are you out of the vision?" Cheryssa says.

"Vision? What vision?" Marrida asks.

"The one you started doing while we were doing the exercise…" Cheryssa says.

"I don't know how to do them…" Marrida protests.

"Until now, maybe not. But you've mastered it…" Cheryssa replies.

"But how…?" Marrida asks.

"I don't know. I'd guess you're among the strongest in a long time, that has existed…" Cheryssa says.

Marrida notices the staring eyes around her. She looks around. She sees eleven people staring back at her, and she sees some girls nudging one another before they whisper to each other. Some girls look like they admire her for what she did, while others do not.

One person looks at Marrida with clear disgust on her face. Marrida's eyes lock for several minutes with Sarayna's eyes, and Marrida genuine feels surprised when it is Sarayna who looks away first.

Marrida looks at Cheryssa. "You say I did a vision. But I don't know if I did…" Marrida tries to sound diplomatic and tries to sound like she genuinely didn't. But deep down, Marrida already knows the answer.

She did a vision and is certain it's the intention of the Elder to show the skill of the girl in the most effective way possible, with an undeniable outcome.

"We will need to discuss the matter with the Elder…" Cheryssa says once more.

Marrida frowns when she hears that. The clear smirk showing

now on Sarayna's face makes her think she's done something seriously wrong. It seems Sarayna found something new to cause annoyance with. But she remembers the words spoken by the Elder.

"How many did a vision too?" she asks.

"Only *two* others. They're going to see the Elder," Cheryssa says, "And those from the other three groups, who did a vision, will go too."

Marrida wonders who else is going and has to suppress a smile when Sarayna isn't one of them.

Cheryssa groups the girls, which includes Marrida by the door. She directs the other girls to the other side of the room, and Marrida notices Cheryssa positioning Sarayna rather forcefully in a position with her back towards Marrida. It hadn't escaped her attention the older woman seems to foster dislike for the younger girl. Cheryssa opens the door, and calls over one Keeper there, explaining in hushed tones about the events, then instructing the Keeper to take the four girls to the Elder. Marrida is introduced to the other girls once they're outside the room and they shut the door. Marrida, Elynna, Caridna and Taryn all smile nervously at one another.

They follow the Keeper, who stays silent during the complete walk to the Elder's chambers. She knocks on the door, and a muffled *"Enter"* can be heard. She opens the door and nods to motion the girls inside. As she enters the room, Marrida catches a glimpse of another group of four girls arriving through the corridor, and they *too* are hushed inside quickly. In the room, Marrida sees one group of four girls arrived before she did.

Another knock on the door announces the last group of four girls…

CHAPTER FIFTEEN

Marrida looks around at all those in the room with her, which seems small with so many there. The Elder sits at a desk and writes the names of each girl as they acknowledge her gaze with a name spoken. She looks up toward a girl, and then each girl instinctively knows to say her name. Marrida says her name as clearly as she can when it's her turn.

Announcing of her name turns a few heads in apparent surprise because it's certain that none here realised of them can be as good at the skill as themselves. Marrida sees a knowing smile flash over the faces of the Elders for a moment.

They select sixteen girls for whatever the Elder planned next, and each feels nervous.

"We now need to determine who of each group, who arrived here, are the two strongest with their skill," Elder Sharriba said, "I'll place one of each group together, then those girls go with each of the four Keepers, who are waiting in the corridor for your next test…"

All the girls look at each other.

"I've listed the names of the girls, who should go in a single group," Sharriba says, "The two strongest come back to me for the *next* test. Those eight get grouped into pairs, and then the strongest will return to me. After that, the two strongest of last four will do their ultimate test with *me*…"

Sharriba looks at each girl for a moment.

"There will be *two* groups. The sixteen who was the strongest, and those not. Those strongest will progress faster to their next stage of learning here," she says.

Marrida wonders in which group she'll be placed, if any.

It seems the Elder is deliberately slow with her selection process, and Marrida actually sees the Elder takes great delight in making the other girls nervous. Marrida feels her own nervousness disappear gradually as the process goes on. She sees the Elder smile knowingly in her direction a few times. At least, she's certain this is the case…

Once the Elder finishes grouping the girls as she wants them, she calls out, and the first of the four Keepers to do the next exercise opens the door and enters the room. Sharriba points at the group she wants to go with the Keeper, and the Keeper leaves, followed by four nervous looking girls.

After about eight minutes four girls, including Marrida, are left with the Elder. She looks at each one, pausing the longest when she looks at Marrida.

"I teach the *best* new Acolytes to join us. I've asked Cheryssa to test the four of you. *Two* of you will be taught later by me personally," Sharriba says.

The girls look at one another. It's some unexpected information. Marrida has to bite her lip to stop herself from grinning. Now, she fully understands what the Elder is doing. She's making sure it appears by chance only that Marrida ended up in this group. Marrida feels like she's part of a conspiracy.

She looks at the Elder and catches her winking. Elder Sharriba gets up and opens the door. Cheryssa enters the room.

"Keeper Cheryssa is most trusted by me personally, so she gets to test the best ones. Those of you who pass *this* test will become an Acolyte," she says, "Please follow her, and I'll join you very soon…"

Marrida looks over her shoulder at the Elder, before leaving the room. It seems to her there's something on the Elder's mind she's trying to suppress. The consequence of becoming a Keeper also makes a person more observant. Without knowing it yet, Marrida starts the process of storing information about the people around her in her memory.

Marrida follows the Keeper and other girls a short distance to another room, where Cheryssa tells them to sit down. She wonders why Cheryssa might be so trusted by the Elder, but decides to assume she'll never be told this information. She looks at the Keeper who's possibly in her thirties, and she has light brown hair, which tumbles down to her shoulders. The Keeper looks at the four girls with dark brown eyes, which are a contrast to her pale skin and her light brown hair. She's tall, but not slender. Marrida decides she likes the woman even more than before.

When Cheryssa looks in her direction, she smiles and feels happy when the Keeper smiles back at her.

"You remember the exercise we did earlier. We're going to repeat that exercise…" Cheryssa says.

The four girls nod. All of them get their gems out and hold it in their left hand in the way they were instructed to do this earlier. This time the task seems easier to Marrida.

She looks up and waits for the next instruction from the Keeper. Before the instructions come, Marrida can already start feeling the warm sensation on the palm of her left hand. She feels surprised. She looks down at her hand and sees the gem has turned a shinier green tint. Marrida's eyes widen with surprise. It isn't what happened before. And this new normal takes Marrida by surprise and makes her feel shocked at the same time.

"Please close your eyes. This time there will be *no* blindfold. I'll check that you're doing the exercise correctly," Cheryssa says.

Marrida shuts her eyes. She waits again for the strange sensations she experienced several times now. The feelings are taxing her young body, but like Cheryssa stated before, she's among the strongest in the skill. She's learning to *do* visions…

First, the now familiar blackness comes. Marrida can't even call it *darkness*. It's *blackness* instead, and even raising her hand just a hand length away from her face, tells her this is a different dark than the dark of night. This dark engulfs all her surroundings, it cushions her; it embraces her. While it also feels scary, it also has a soothing feeling to it at the same time. It's the same sensation as she felt before when she was instructed to hold the gem when meeting the Elder.

The same sensation she'd felt earlier when she was told she, in fact, did a vision. Marrida feels the change before it starts.

A new sensation courses through her body, leaving her gasping for air. In front of her, Cheryssa sits down on a stool and watches the girl's behaviour closely. She whispers to the other girls to remain silent. They glance at one another, each having the telling expression of *"How?"* on their faces. Some of them have been at the Temple for months now, and none of them has ever witnessed the progress of attunement happen so fast before.

They know what the exercise really means. It means that after today, this girl is like them. She, too, can do visions, even it's under the strict supervision of a Keeper or the Elder…

CHAPTER SIXTEEN

Marrida knows *this* time the exercise has a different outcome than those she did before. This time, she seems to be pulled into whatever it is she is experiencing, and however she tried, she has no way to remove herself from it. She looks around and notices the blackness around her clears up. She notices her surroundings. She sees a table first. Then sees a window. And then a chair becomes visible. Gradually a room comes into view, and it isn't the same room as she saw before.

Whereas the earlier room she saw was well decorated, this room feels sparse. And from how it appears, it's clear the occupier of it liked it to be in this way.

Marrida tries to make sense of why she sees this room and place of all places. It feels familiar, like she should know it from somewhere.

Where am I?

No answer comes. She seems alone in this place, which causes her to wonder if she's imagined the voices in the earlier visions. She shakes her head, trying to remove the idea from her mind. It worries her. She breathes in deep, then makes use of the opportunity, because she thought perhaps Cheryssa might want to know what she is seeing.

She doesn't know yet that Cheryssa and the three girls next to her all are watching her vision unfolding itself in a disc-shape that has formed itself a few minutes earlier. They see everything Marrida observes inside the vision she's doing. And the girls around Cheryssa are very intrigued by what they see. None of them has done a proper vision yet, and this is their first experience of one. And two of the girls even feel admiration for the much younger girl for not giving up when there's obvious animosity towards her.

The third girl, who felt the need to be on friendly terms with Sarayna, now feels shame for her earlier behaviour. But she was warned by Sarayna *not* to be too friendly with this girl, or there would be consequences for her instead.

Temerin, the girl in question, is one year older than Marrida, and she realises deep down that she, and not Marrida, could have been the youngest girl there. Secretly, she admires the younger girl and is nice to her when they're alone. She knows Marrida has a brother and sister and finds out more about them, too.

She saw Marrida talk to a boy who seems to be eleven or twelve years, and who looks like her. She finds out more about the boy, because if he's as nice as some say, then she might have found the person to consider later as a life partner if she doesn't get to be an Acolyte or a Keeper…

Marrida investigates what she sees in the vision, blissfully unaware of the various emotions she stirs around her. She sees the vision as her chance to disprove what Sarayna said to her. In a big way, she's right. It's planting the seeds of doubt in the hearts of those who believed the rumour Sarayna spoke, but there's a side effect to what's happening Marrida won't know about until much later.

Something about the setting feels odd to Marrida. She's seen no place that looks like it, and she constantly fights the urge to assume this place is one she knows. She makes mental notes of what she sees so she can describe it later. The room is small, and she sees a stairway that leads to somewhere upstairs. She notices voices coming from there, although she can't make out who speaks and what about. And because she doesn't know how to move from the place she stands, she can't go to find out either.

She can determine it is two women speaking.

No, it seems a woman and a girl.

But they speak *too* soft for Marrida determine what their dialect might be. It seems their conversation is so private, that they're doing their best also to deny history from being able to ascertain its content. So, Marrida does a different task. She makes mental notes so she can tell her experience in detail.

First, she looks at the table. It's plain looking. But it serves its function. On it lies a partially cut loaf of bread, with next to it several slices. A bite from one slice indicates someone was sitting at the table not so long ago, eating it. The reason why they got up is unclear. She stares at the table. Something is so familiar about it, and the room she's in, that she lets out a cursing in the way she'd heard her uncle do occasionally. She doesn't realise she does it vocally, and that Keeper Cheryssa frowns for a moment, and the surrounding girls suppress an urge to giggle…

Marrida hears someone laugh behind her. For a moment she thinks she's left her vision and is being teased by one of her tormentors, but this laughter is a delightful laughter of someone who's discovered something humorous. It takes much willpower to turn around. She sees a girl who's perhaps a year, maybe two years younger than Kalisa. It isn't Kalisa because this girl has darker hair. Someone near speaks, and the girl laughs once more.

Marrida realises she's, in fact, seeing an event from an unknown past of someone… somewhere…

She decides she's probably being tested for something Elder Sharriba is doing, or perhaps plans to do soon. She wants to see more stuff, but she realises another sensation. This sensation isn't something she's been told or explained about. While Marrida's vision is ongoing, Sharriba has arrived, and after observing the vision for a few minutes, decides it's enough. She brings the girl out of the vision.

Cheryssa looks puzzled at the Elder for her abrupt behaviour. She isn't known for bringing any potential Acolyte from a vision so soon, and so abruptly. Elder Sharriba knows what Marrida saw. It's a distant and hidden past she keeps from everyone, and even from herself. She knows Marrida will want to speak to her about what she saw. Her mind is in turmoil about what she saw.

I wish my mother hadn't done that.

Sharriba dismisses the thought from her mind. She swallows

hard, trying to kerb her emotions. She concentrates on the girl to make sure she's alright. The girl's swaying shows she's almost out of the vision.

"I'm thirsty…" Marrida says in a croaky voice. She feels a cup being pushed in her hands.

"The first vision can disorient…" a voice says.

Marrida recognises it as the Elder's voice.

She frowns when she hears it, but hides her concerned frown by drinking the cool water.

CHAPTER SEVENTEEN

Marrida glances around, then she asks, "What happened?"

"You did a vision…" The answer comes from one girl, who doesn't even flinch by speaking out of turn. Marrida looks at the girl and is met by awe, and it surprises her. She next looks again at the Elder, still wondering what her comment means.

"You did a vision but… It isn't important what the vision showed. It's more important to know that you *can* do visions," Elder Sharriba admonishes.

I wonder why not? Marrida thinks, but she says nothing.

Instead, she sips a few more times from the cup, while she thinks about the vision. She wonders who the little girl she saw in the vision might be, and even more, what the significance is between it, and the comment from the Elder, that it isn't important.

If the Elder was in the room long enough for her to see it, then she might know who the girl was. It's a mystery to solve for later.

Marrida already wonders if she can repeat the exercise, or more precisely the vision when she's home and alone in her sleeping room.

"I think I'm alright now…" she puts the cup down beside her.

"Good, I think you've demonstrated the skill, so, therefore, you'll pass to the next phase of training, and in another season or so, you'll be made an Acolyte," Sharriba says.

"How long does the training take?" Marrida decides to pretend the conversation between the Elder and herself, privately conducted, never happened. It seems the Elder understands what Marrida is doing, and she responds in kind.

"It takes anything from a half-decade to slightly more than a decade *before* you become a Keeper. Even then training never stops," Sharriba says.

"I'm still learning new things from the many books," Cheryssa says.

"And even I learn new things every day," Sharriba says. Marrida looks from Sharriba to Cheryssa and back to Sharriba. It's obvious from what they say that being a Keeper is a lifelong commitment. But Sharriba stated her mother was a Keeper, and that she gave it up to become her father's life partner. If that's the case, then it brings with it another dilemma.

As young as she is, Marrida already decided long ago she wants to have a relationship with someone, just in the same way her parents had when they both still lived. If what's said about her mother is true, it meant she needs to make a choice between being a Keeper and or being a life partner of someone. She frowns when she realises. Elder Sharriba guesses what the girl is thinking about and has to contain her emotions once more because of it. She has secrets she can't share with anyone, not even Marrida who has won her trust already…

Marrida watches as Temerin is instructed in the same way as Marrida to repeat the exercises, and then Marrida gets a glimpse of what those in the room witnessed. She sees a disc-shaped form itself to Temerin's right and sees an image form itself within it. Marrida sees a tall man, who bears a striking resemblance to Temerin, and Marrida guesses that's some sort of family member of the girl. When the man picks up a very young girl, only just past the first formative years of her life, and lifts the girl through the air which invites an outburst of giggles from her, it's clear to Marrida that Temerin is doing a vision of herself as a young child.

Then who did I do a vision of? Marrida thinks again, *why couldn't I do something of my past?*

Seeing the vision of Temerin with her father brings a flood of emotion to Marrida because it causes her to realise how much she misses her parents. But watching Temerin's vision also gives her a greater understanding of her own skill, which is as good or perhaps better than Temerin's skill seems to be. Temerin's vision ends a moment later, and it makes Marrida wonder how long her own vision lasted.

The visions shown by the other two girls have varying levels of success to it. They each show things that matter to them. Marrida enjoys seeing glimpses of the girls' family lives. It makes her appreciate even more the few years she had with her own parents. After they did all of their visions, the girls get paired up. Marrida and Temerin walk with Elder Sharriba to another room, where she sits them down, and then sits waiting silently.

After about fifteen minutes, two of the girls from another group enter the room, and Sharriba motions them to the bench where Marrida and Temerin are sitting. The four girls all look at each other and smile nervously at one another. They look at the Elder, who looks at each.

"I'm going to teach the four of you the skills that will make you an Acolyte before they complete three seasons. After that, your formal education here starts, and when that happens, you'll learn a range of different parts of knowledge," Sharriba explains.

The four girls all nod, all feeling tongue-tied because they're now certain they passed the tests of the day. Marrida wonders who of the other girls who started today, will also pass the tests, and therefore also become Acolytes. Marrida guesses they'd know later in the day. Marrida suddenly wonders how late in the day it is, because she did so much, and she did the vision too, so she feels she has lost track of time.

Elder Sharriba talks in detail about the various skills and knowledge the girls are to learn in the next two years. The list seems endless to Marrida. And she is certain the lessons with the Elder are besides this.

Another hour passes, then Elder Sharriba announces that it's time for the girls to go home. She warns them *not* to speak about their new status or anything else they learn in the Temple. All four of them nod in response, and Marrida feels the Elder looks at her longer than all the other girls. Luckily, it seems they notice nothing going on between the Elder and Marrida.

In the vestibule, Temerin quickly rushes to the group standing around Sarayna, who gives Marrida an angry stare, but this time none of them speak to her. Marrida glances around, and wonders if Sarayna isn't doing any of her usual taunts because of the presence of the Elder and Keepers in the vestibule.

Marrida turns, and quickly departs, and walks fast to make sure she gets as close to home *before* Sarayna notices she's left the Temple…

CHAPTER EIGHTEEN

Marrida walks into the front room when she hears Kalisa giggle. Here she finds Kalisa, Esbara, and a boy she doesn't immediately recognise.

"Marrida, this is Damir," Kalisa says as she hurls herself against her sister for a hug, "He came to deliver some food supplies from uncle…"

Marrida raises her left hand in the customary greeting, and Damir copies her action. He glances at Esbara, who nods.

"I was told you wanted to see my drawings…" he says.
"Yes, I did…" Marrida replies.
"I got a drawing in my knapsack…" Damir says, grinning. He opens the knapsack and pulls out a slender tube.

Damir unties some soft cords on one end, then tips it and a roll of Joharan's familiar parchment slides from the container.

Damir puts the tube down on the seating beside him, then carefully unrolls the parchment and places it on the table in front of it, and holds the edges to keep it from rolling back up. Esbara holds one further corner, and Kalisa takes hold of the remaining corner.

Marrida looks closely at the drawing, comparing it with the painting on the wall.

"It's beautiful…" she looks at the painting on the wall, and asks, "Did you draw it from memory, from what Kalisa described?"

Damir nods.

"I like it…" Kalisa says.
"Then, if it's alright with Damir, we'll get it hung in your

room…" Marrida suggests.

"I did it for Kalisa…" Damir says.

Marrida glances over at the boy. She wonders about the statement. She glances at Kalisa and sees her sister turn a shade of red because of it. She smiles inwardly.

He's already decided about who he wants as a life partner as young as he is.

It makes her wonder if she'll ever meet someone to have a similar opportunity with.

"Joharan told us the retelling about these animals," Damir smiles, "He says there are maybe a few left in the east, but most of them were killed a thousand years ago or before that…"

"Yes, it's a pity so few exist now. And even fewer every year," Marrida says.

"I think it's the Wolf Riders who hunt the last of them," Damir says, "And they kill the parents, and their offspring is often unable to defend itself against an ailep hound that wants to hunt for its next meal…"

"Have you seen an ailep hound?" Esbara asks.

"Yes, a few times." Damir doesn't add he secretly hunts them but sees from Esbara's face the other boy suspects this might be the case.

He changes the subject.

"Joharan wants to visit a village to the southeast where they grow rubha apples," he says, "Apparently, a merchant there asked for him, and he wants to discuss a new trading agreement with him. Joharan already told me I can go with him there, and before I came here, he stated I should tell you *all* that you, too, are going with him. We're leaving in ten days from now, and we'll be *there* for half a season. He said… errr… Marrida, he told me you work at the Temple cleaning it. He said to me to tell you to mention to them you won't be there for a few weeks…"

Marrida looks at the boy with an abrupt jerk of her head. She hadn't mentioned to her siblings what exactly she does at the Temple, but he has put it out in the open.

But she's glad he said what he said because it means her uncle had believed Sharriba, when she stated the girl was going to be a servant at the Temple, and not the Keeper she's training for…

"I must ask permission there before I can decide whether to go, but Kalisa and Esbara can go," Marrida knows her uncle, and not she, is ultimately the one who decides, but she wants to vocalise her thoughts, anyway.

If they go and I don't, then I have the house to myself for half a season, and therefore the ability to practise the skills I learnt today. Maybe if I mention it, but claim to the Elder I don't want to get her to say something that makes it impossible for me to go, it would help too…

Marrida asks about the retelling Joharan told the boy and listens to it. Some of it. She remembers from being told it by her uncle, but she thinks her uncle has gone into greater detail with Damir than he ever did with his own niece. A lot of the retelling intrigues her, and she notices she's paying very close attention to remember the details of it better. She's certain she might get to hear the retelling directly told by her uncle, one day…

Marrida gets up. "I had a long day of work today," she says, "I'm tired. I think I'll lie down until we have the evening meal."

She walks from the front room before either sibling or Damir can respond.

Marrida pauses a moment at the stairway before climbing it. She feels tired, but *not* from work, but from the intensity of the exercises involving the beginning of becoming an Acolyte. The Elder stated the final decision who'll learn as Acolyte would be made the next day. She hopes she's one of them, but she remembers the words of the Elder, that she has to wait two or three seasons before she can start.

She wonders if it's possible to be selected as Acolyte and still be a Temple Maiden for a period…

Marrida thinks about what Damir stated about a planned journey with her uncle. It will happen in ten days from now, and one way or another she needs to make sure she stays home during the trip even if her uncle disapproves.

But she wants to see the region he plans to visit.

Marrida reaches up to the gem hanging from a golden chain. She wonders if the retelling from the Elder about the origin of the gem's name is really true, or if it's all just a retelling…

I can test it one day while I'm busy in the cooking room. If I put the gem among the apples, and Kalisa and Esbara both come into the room, and neither notices the gem, then I know Elder Sharriba spoke the truth…

CHAPTER NINETEEN

Marrida sits down on her bed and sighs. She hadn't lied when she had said that she was feeling tired, but she feels guilty about the reason. She just can't disobey the rules of the Temple. She pulls the gem from under her tunic and stares at it for a while.

Can I do a vision all by myself, even though it is forbidden?

She determines the only way to find out is to do a vision. She places the gem on the bed, gets up, and walks to the door. She opens the door a moment to listen to the sounds of her siblings and Damir talking, then she shuts the door, and like a few days earlier locks it. She waits at the door to thinking a moment.

I'm curious about the vision the Elder dismissed so quickly. But I rather would try to see more of the lives of my parents...

She turns and walks to the bed, and after a pause, she sits down. She looks around the room, remembering whose room this was before she used it. She feels a lump in her throat from the emotions.

"I miss you both so much..." she whispers.

Marrida picks up the gem and again wonders what vision to do if she can get one going. She thinks for a few minutes about the exercises she did that day. She wonders for a moment if the Elder somehow knew she did visions by herself. Marrida shakes her head.

She can only see past events as a Keeper. She can't know what Marrida might do in the future.

Marrida looks down at the gem which belonged to her mother. According to lessons with Sharriba, it was passed down from mother to daughter, and this went on for many generations already. She wonders about her maternal grandmother. She doesn't know anything about her, but as her mother came from Marridina, Marrida is certain her maternal grandmother lives there or perhaps had lived there.

She knows even less about her paternal grandparents, so she can't even imagine who *they* were. She knows both of them are dead because her uncle told her that. She knows her father was her uncle's younger brother.

Neither of them ever spoke of anyone who's *their* paternal or maternal grandparents.

But then who is that old woman I saw?

Marrida raises her left hand and stares for a while at the lines in her palm. After a hesitation, she places the gem on her palm, then looks at her hand with the gem lying on it for a while. She moves her hand closer to her body, so it is positioned in the manner Keeper Cheryssa instructed her to hold it. Marrida stares and waits. Nothing happens. For a moment, Marrida wonders what she might do wrong. Then she remembers…

She looks around the room one more time, then looks down at the gem, then shut her eyes. She waits. She senses the change sooner than during the exercise. She feels a glow of warmth in her left palm, and instinctively places her right hand above the gem, not quite touching it but almost.

She senses a presence. She's certain it's the beginning of the vision. After several minutes, the urge to open her eyes becomes too great, and she opens them. She feels surprised when she's met by the same blackness from before. Then after a few more minutes, it clears up, and she starts to sense her surroundings have altered. She's surprised to find herself standing in the middle of her uncle's courtyard adjoining his workshop. She looks around; wondering *why* she's here of all places; wondering if thinking about her grandparents, who lived here before they died, has something to do with her being *here*.

She hears voices, then a child's laughter, and it sounds so familiar to her ears. She turns to see where it comes from and is surprised to see a girl of around six years old, who pulls a sack along the ground, obviously on the instruction of the deep voice she'd heard moments before. She smiles…

At least now, she has a glimpse of family memories, like Temerin and the other two girls, even if it's one of her with her uncle and not the one she'd hoped for. Marrida starts moving forward towards the scene, but before she manages to take no more than ten steps closer, darkness encloses her again. When it clears up, she sees a scene that's equally familiar, but for entirely other reasons.

These reasons are unpleasant ones. The reason she and Esbara are at loggerheads about *his* choice to want to become a soldier of the city. This part of the vision shows her why…

This is when they came. This is four years ago…

She remembers the day *well*. She'd been visiting her uncle. But later in that day, turmoil had struck the city, and it was Marrida's first encounter with the menace that exists in Keldarra; which her uncle had carefully protected her against until then…

Kalisa had only just walked and at age seven Esbara was *still* too young to understand fully what's going on. But Marrida was old enough. When she was urged home by her uncle, Esbara had said he wanted to see the soldiers in action. They were almost home when he rushed off running in the gatehouse's direction, leaving Marrida feeling in a state of panic. She was responsible for her siblings and had been so since their parents died a few years earlier.

It was evening when Esbara finally returned home, covered from head to toe in the soot from the fires that broke out in the city. She was fuming mad at him, and when he'd raised his voice at her, she'd screamed at him, "They'll snatch you if you're in the streets…"

Marrida shakes her head. This isn't the memory she wants to see, and with an enormous amount of willpower, she finally breaks free from the vision.

She slumps on the bed for a moment, breathing deep, almost panting like she's been running a long distance.

She reaches for her cup and the jug of water beside it. She pours in water, drinks it down fast, then fills a second and then a third cup full she drank as hastily.

Why is she always so thirsty after a vision…?

Marrida wonders if every vision is going to be like this, but to know the answer means going to the Temple, and asking Elder Sharriba. She knows she can't do that. It's forbidden…

Tomorrow I'll work hard on learning as much as I can, so I do these visions easier…

CHAPTER TWENTY

Marrida walks through the street towards her uncle's house. Her plan to visit the Temple today had been altered by Damir's arrival very early in the morning with the message from Joharan, and he'd explained their uncle needs to speak to them. She wonders if this conversation is about the journey he had planned.

Marrida, Esbara and Kalisa arrive at the door of Joharan's house, and Marrida opens the door immediately.

Inside they find Joharan sitting at the table in the cooking room, with Damir sitting opposite him eating a morning meal, which he had to forgo earlier in the morning to deliver the message. Joharan smiles when he sees the trio and holds his arms apart when Kalisa gives him a hug. She climbs on his lap and puts her arms around his neck. He squeezes the tiny girl in his broad arms until she giggles with delight.

It makes Marrida smile because there was a time she'd have done the same…

"Marrida, apparently, I can't take you with me on my journey, at least *not* for the entire period," Joharan says, "Apparently, in a season from now, you'll start working as a permanent Temple Maiden. The appointment up to now was just temporary…"

Marrida frowns for a moment, then sets her face to a neutral stance, so her uncle won't notice her confusion.

She wonders why he'd get a message from Elder Sharriba.

Why didn't Sharriba just wait to tell me when she gets to the Temple?

"Because of that, I've went on this journey sooner. We're leaving in *two* days from now," Joharan continues.

"Where are we going?" Kalisa grins broadly with excitement about the prospect of a journey.

"We're going to see where they grow the apples," Joharan answers.

"Sooo… we need to pack clothing and such, to bring with us," Kalisa says.

"That's right. We'll be visiting a merchant I know in the region, so you can just bring summer clothing," Joharan says.

"How long are we going to be there?" Esbara notices something odd about Marrida's reaction, that she's less enthusiastic than he might expect her to be.

"We're visiting there for twenty days," Joharan answers, "Only that long because it will give us enough time to travel back home before Marrida starts her work as Temple Maiden…"

"Will there be anyone I can play with?" Kalisa asks.

"Of course, my friend has a granddaughter the *same* age as you. I'm sure you two will be good friends, and have a lot of fun together," Joharan says.

"Oooh… nice…" Kalisa bounces with excitement on Joharan's lap.

"Calm down, or you'll break the chair I'm sitting on…" Joharan chides Kalisa.

She stops bouncing, curls her lip in annoyance for a moment, then grins again, but now leans against her uncle's chest, and lets his massive arms envelop her.

Marrida silently watches the interaction between her uncle and her younger sister. She feels a bit of sadness she's almost considered a young adult and therefore climbing on the lap of a favourite uncle would be seen as odd. But, she vows to let her sister have as much time as possible she can give her to feel wanted and loved by her uncle.

"I wasn't aware that they had selected me for the work as a Temple Maiden," Marrida says softly in a voice that she tries to make the sound as neutral as she could.

"I received a letter from the Elder last night. They gave a patrolling city guardsman it as he passed the Temple. They instructed him to bring it to me immediately," Joharan replies, "I sent Damir early, so he could get you to come here before you might have left for the Temple. Apparently, you're not needed there today, as they're now selecting the second group of Temple Maidens…"

Marrida frowns because now she's uncertain what her uncle refers to.

"It means you can stay here, so take off your cloak and sit down," Joharan says, unaware of the confusion Marrida feels.

Esbara and Damir look at one another with knowing glances. They noticed Marrida's behaviour. But neither of them says a word, and they try to pretend they're none the wiser.

"Damir, can you bring three more bowls, and put the pot of honey porridge on the table, and go get a fresh jug of milk from storage," Joharan says. Damir gets up and quickly complies with his mentor's request.

As he walks past Joharan, he smiles at Kalisa who smiles back for a moment, then she becomes shy and buries her face against Joharan's chest. Damir decides he likes her even more than before, especially after watching her interaction with her uncle. He walks from the room, but as he does that, Kalisa glances up and looks at him until he turns a corner.

I like him. Kalisa thinks.

Minutes later, she sees Damir returning with a heavy jug.

* * *

Marrida takes her cloak off and drapes it over the chair near the front door. She slides on the bench next to Esbara, while Damir sits back down on the other side. Kalisa climbs off Joharan's lap and sits down opposite of Marrida, and when the two sisters catch each other's eyes, they smile at one another. Marrida feels a warmth of happiness wash over her. This is the day she enjoys the most.

But she knows those days are numbered now…

Marrida is distracted, so she doesn't notice the bowl of porridge being passed in her direction until Esbara nudges her in the ribs. For a moment, she looks annoyed at her brother, then takes the bowl being held out to her.

She smiles at her uncle, now grateful to him, and the Elder too, that for a while she can forgo seeing those at the Temple who wish her ill feelings…

CHAPTER TWENTY ONE

Marrida feels upset, finally arriving back at Joharan's house, after twenty days of visiting the orchards in the southeast area of Sabeya. Tomorrow, she'd have to go back to the Temple…

Marrida is already sure that Sarayna has spread a rumour that they expelled Marrida. Returning means Sarayna has renewed fuel for tormenting her, and this time about the fact that Marrida apparently *only* is a Temple Maiden, and not fit for training to be a Keeper. She isn't even sure if Sarayna is any good at her skill…

She waits until she's alone with her uncle, then she speaks. "Uncle Joharan, I need to talk to you about something…"

He nods at the table, the customary place he'd sit to listen to discuss things with those around him.

"I don't know how things will *be* at the Temple, while I work there," she says, "There's this girl there who seems to dislike me, and she seems to know about you…"

"What has she said?" Joharan asks.

Before Marrida can answer, Esbara, Kalisa and Damir walk in, and their arrival startles Marrida somewhat. She looks down at the table, and she refuses to answer her uncle's last question.

"Please, go outside," Joharan says sternly, "I have a matter to discuss with Marrida…"

The three youngsters turn without saying a word and go back the way they just came from. Damir shuts the door behind him as he's the last to leave.

"She said… she said I don't belong there. She says you're not my proper father. That you don't care about me at all," Marrida answers then she bursts out crying.

"I care about you. A lot," Joharan places a gentle hand over Marrida's hand. She looks up at Joharan and receives a gentle smile back. "How did it all start?" he asks next.

"It started the first day I went there," Marrida says, "I wasn't nice to Kalisa before it happened, and I feel upset and guilty for it…"

"She's your sister. She'll forgive whatever happened *that* day…" Joharan says.

"I hope so. I really love her…" Marrida says, and she lets out a sob.

"Who's the girl who doesn't seem to like you?" Joharan asks, but before Marrida can answer, there's a knock on the door leading to the back courtyard.

"Yes…?" Joharan calls out.

Damir opens the door. "May I go with Kalisa and Esbara to their house?" he asks, "I promised Esbara I'd help him in the garden…"

"Yes, yes… You can have free time…" Joharan says.

The door opens wider and the three youngsters walk in. Kalisa rushes to Joharan to give him a hug before she follows her brother and Damir to the front door.

"Damir shut the curtain please before you go…" Joharan calls out.

Damir does as he was instructed, though his glance at Marrida makes it clear that he wonders what his mentor and Marrida are discussing, that warrants a sign to show that Joharan is not to be disturbed by any. He doesn't ask, and a moment later, he shuts and locks the door behind him, before he follows the other two youngsters quickly through the street to their house.

"She said I'm too young to be there…"

"The Elder doesn't think so…" Joharan replies.

"But why am I told to be a Temple Maiden then…?"

"That's something you should ask *her*. I don't know. But you're less than a year from First Rites, and then you *are* a young adult. Then, you share responsibility for your siblings with *me*," Joharan says, "When it happens, no one can tell you that you're too young. You'll grow up soon enough. You'll pass your Second Rites before you even know it…"

Marrida nods, then she wipes the tears from her wet cheeks. "I guess so," she says softly.

"I know so," Joharan says. "Come here, and I'll give you a cuddle. I saw you were looking at Kalisa when she hugged me with such longing in your eyes…"

Marrida gets up, though, feeling self-conscious and somewhat hesitant. She senses it's regarded as inappropriate to start climbing on her uncle's lap.

But he taps the seat beside him. She sits down, and he puts his arm around her shoulders, and although he squeezes her closer to him, he allows her the dignity of feeling grown up enough to sit beside him.

"While we're on our next journey, I'll teach you some more of my skills at the same time as I teach them to Damir."

Joharan kisses Marrida's forehead. Marrida nods and looks up, smiling at her uncle. She wonders what skills it will be, but guesses it will be something to serve useful for the rest of her life.

"I love you, Uncle Joharan…"

"And I love *you*, Marrida Kayrsan, daughter of my brother, whom I'm certain *you* still miss," Joharan replies.

"I do still miss Papa. And Mam too…"

"I miss them both *too*…" Joharan says.

Both of them look up, surprised at the sound echoing across the city.

"I think you best go home. The gong is being sounded. There might be an attack on its way."

Marrida nods and puts her cloak on in readiness to go home.

Joharan stops her, then gives her advice Marrida will remember for all the years to come.

"Marrida, remember *this* lesson. It's those who bully others, who have the misfortune of losing out. You're a *good* person," Joharan says, "Future events *will* show you that…"

Marrida nods, then she hugs her uncle. He lifts her head and kisses her forehead before speaking one more time.

"As for this girl called Sarayna. I think she'll be the one left feeling afraid, in the end. When *she* forgets a gesture of kindness shown to her, after *that* you'll feel so much stronger than she is. All the things she did or said, won't matter to you anymore when you discover that strength," Joharan says, "Now *go* home, and all of you stay indoors. Tell Damir to *stay* there with you until it's over, then to return *here* when it's safe again…"

Marrida rushes home, lifting her skirt so she can run most of the way.

She doesn't know yet that less than half a decade later she'd be repeating this same action for entirely other reasons. As she runs through the streets, that is emptying fast, Marrida has a feeling deep down something profound has started when she joined the Order of Truth.

Something that will forever alter her life. In what way is something she doesn't know yet…

91

Alagur

CHAPTER ONE

"There's the legend of the first wolves, the invaders from the north mastered," Elder Man Vaymaz hisses, which he knows to capture the attention of the boys sitting around him, Alagur among them, "One among them, they named Mountain Ghost, because this wolf was even larger than most of those wolves. These wolves are already larger than most wolves, such as the ailep hounds of the east…"

Alagur is older than most of the boys surrounding the Elder Man, but he's the most captive of them all, and the Elder Man can see it in the boy's face. This boy intrigues the old man. Something about him is different compared to almost all others in the city. This boy is quieter, he never vies for favours from the Elder Men.

Looking at the boy, the Elder Man can see that he plans something with the information he learnt from the stories…

"Mountain Ghost lived a thousand or so years ago. He was a wolf that came from the highest peaks of Northern Blades. Those mountains are some of the highest that exists in Keldarra," Vaymaz says, "And they are treacherous, cold, it will cause ice burn, and there are many wolves there…"

Vaymaz looks directly at Alagur. He sees the boy frown and then looks away like they have caught him in a secret. He's certain that Alagur plans something daring. He has to admit to himself *this* boy of all boys going after a wolf that's of the same breed as Mountain Ghost, is possibly one of the most courageous things ever done by *any* boy. He knows that most of the Elder Men around him don't agree with the ideas he has for these boys. Having one among them, who's going to defy the will of the Wolf Riders so openly, is perhaps a good sign for the future. Secretly he hopes the boy will succeed because if he does, it will set in motion something that only two other Elder Men believe to be the future…

Alagur sits staring in the distance, thinking about the wolf he'll get for himself. He doesn't notice the old man observing him intently for a time, before the old man turns and walks off.

A few moments later, a hand slaps hard across the back of the boy's head, which causes the dreams of wolf bonding from his mind momentarily.

"Ouch…" Alagur yells involuntarily.

"Get to work, you lazy runt…" Darush says, and he's met by an angry stare from Alagur. Darush has arrived only months earlier, and it seems to him this man is somehow best friends with Samur, who'd claimed a number of times that Alagur is his pack brother. Alagur grumbles an inaudible cursing under his breath and quickly walks off to the building where he's supposed to help with weapon making. He walks into the building to be greeted by another slap over his head.

"You're late again…" Elder Man Edgryn makes clear he isn't pleased about a boy's behaviour, "I should throw you in the pits and see how you like that…"

Edgryn laughs loud, watching Alagur rush quickly to the back corner of the room where the boy sits down beside two other boys, who look at him with as much disdain as Edgryn does while the boy walked from him.

Alagur picks up the few dozens of metal staves which, he was told, are for the siege weaponry they're going to use against a city to the northeast of City of the Wolves. He doesn't know the name of the city, but it's apparent from the conversations he overheard, that the attacks are frequent, that they've become more frequent in recent years.

From the whispers of other boys, he understands the man to be responsible for the increase in attacks to be the man he calls friend and brother: Samur.

I wonder if Samur is getting other boys from that city. He spoke of a city further north. He said he plans to go that later. I don't like it here. I wish I was back home with Mam and Papa, and my little sister, She called after me, I think. I wonder why…

Alagur picks up several more of the metal staves and places them on the bench in distances of one hand width apart. He picks up a container which he knows to contain pitch. Using a leather scrap, he brushes the foul-smelling substance on the surface of the staves. He isn't sure what the reason for it is, but it's apparently going to be a weapon of some sort… or so Samur says.

One day I'll have my wolf. I'll ride it and I won't do this awful smelling work. One day it will be me, who's ordering a boy to do all this for me…

Alagur glances at Edgryn, who stands at the door, leaning against its side, behaving like he's the most important person there.

I reckon he was doing this work when he was thirty or forty years younger. A few years more, and he'll be gone…

Alagur spends the next three hours doing the same laborious, and rather repetitive work of preparing the staves, until a nod from the Elder Man dismisses him. As he rushes past the man, he gets another slap across the back of his head…

Alagur walks to his sleeping house, and as he enters it, he sees he's there alone. He walks to a low, wide bench that has to resemble a bed. He sits down, and looks around for a few minutes, and listens to determine he is alone there. After being certain he's alone, he pulls a small knapsack from under the bench. For a moment, he stops with what he's doing when he hears some voices outside, but they fade after a few minutes. If he wants to go, he must do things fast, and be certain he's not seen by anyone…

"I wonder if Vaymaz knows what I'm planning…" Alagur wonders for a few moments, then he shakes his head.

The Elder Man is strange, perhaps even enigmatic, but he doesn't give any clues ever: he's anything more than a man past his prime, and therefore not an active Wolf Rider…

Alagur waits until an hour after dusk, which is when the boys of his sleeping house are called away to have a meal. In the chaos ensuing from having that many boys in one place, it will be an hour or more before anyone will realise he's missing. He has to be out of the city and be at least an hour or more away.

He knows where he wants to go…

CHAPTER TWO

Alagur looks over his shoulder to make sure the alleyway is clear in the other direction. He sees a few boys rushing past in the distance rushing to the main square where food is being served out. Most, if not all, of the Elder Men, will already be on the square, helping themselves to the best helpings of the food. Alagur fights the hunger he feels, suddenly. He can hunt for something outside the city, then eat while travelling. He looks at the buildings he passes, and wonders if he might find something to eat besides what he plans to hunt...

Alagur walks again. He's only four hundred paces from the eastern gatehouse, or at least what's left over of it. He needs to get past that, then he can set off at a sprint, going first towards the lake he was told is called Ribbon Lake. After that, he has to head north towards the Northern Blades. Somewhere where he might find the wolves. He takes an hour, just to get to the nearest woodland, mostly because he stops all the time to make sure no one follows him. Each time, he kneels under the bushes. Before he can go, he has to make sure he's alone.

Good, they'll just think I'm late for the meal. I think the plan for the last few days was a good one...

Alagur thinks he's clever by always being late everywhere, and this isn't being noticed. One Elder Man notices. He discusses the matter with *two* others, who also become intrigued about this boy. They discuss the matter in private and decide they have to observe the boy's actions... using somewhat unusual methods. The boy, Alagur, doesn't know this about these three Elder Men, or he may have paid better attention to their actions. All he sees, as he watches the ancient derelict city, is that for once none of the signal fires are burning. He rarely believes in luck, so to him, it's just chance this is happening at the same time as him wanting to leave the city to get his wolf.

Like all other boys, he is so conditioned to the life of becoming a Wolf Rider, that it never even occurs to him, that this opportunity to leave might also get him home. Something compels him to stay, and it isn't the possibility of getting a wolf, which is its cause…

After fifteen minutes waiting for any of the eastern and northeastern signal fires to be ignited, Alagur's shoulders slump, and tension leaves his body. He straightens up slowly, and turns as slowly, always gazing at the gates of the city for signs of anyone who might search for him. Deep in his heart, he knows the reason he's so cautious now. It's the careless, almost reckless disobedience that had cost him a normal life with his parents and sister.

Alagur knows he misses his family, even so, his mind doesn't realise his departure from the city also can mean his freedom to go home. Somehow, and for an unknown reason, he feels he has a goal to stay in the ranks of the Wolf Riders. Something will happen, and he has to be there to be part of it.

But right now, he just wants to get the wolf. He wants to get his very own Mountain Ghost…

He isn't entirely certain in what part of Northern Blades the wolves are located, but Alagur knows now he's defied the order not to seek them out, he has to return with one or there will be consequences. He swallows hard when it dawns on him the most severe of the punishments is the pit of wild wolves…

Alagur looks up at the sky. He sees the first stars appear, and he knows, by now, he'll be missed for certain. He starts to walk through the undergrowth, walking away from the city as fast as he can. As he walks, he pushes branches aside. He isn't certain of what the landscape has in store for him between here and his destination.

But caution sets in, because of the encroaching darkness around him. It's the first time he's been alone in the dark of night, and it makes his heart pound in his throat. He stops every time he heard a sound, even mistaking his own heartbeat for a sound of someone else being there…

He listens for birds giving signs they're in distress. A bird calls out a warning if a predator of some sort is near. He's certain he can kill any animal that means him harm. He's rather proficient already at killing ailep hounds, which seem to amuse most of the Wolf Riders, and even some younger Elder Men, who still can appreciate the virtues of being a hunter.

Alagur listens for the distinct snarls of ailep hounds, although he isn't certain he can kill one of these animals, let alone several if they are roaming for something to scavenge. He looks around for any pieces of wood that can serve as a stave, even if it isn't the most efficient way of hunting these types of animals. He knows a more efficient way to hunt them, comes when he has a wolf. But that's only if he can bond with one properly…

Alagur stops when he sees some branches that will suit his needs. It will take some effort to remove the straightest of the branches, but he has to kill at least one. He needs food. Water is pretty easy to find, but eating is another matter. And he's been stupid in that he didn't bring any food with him from City of Wolves as that's possibly easier than going hunting with very inadequate weaponry.

After cutting through the wood for well over twenty minutes, Alagur finally can break it off. The wood breaks in two with a snapping sound, which sounds so loud to him, that Alagur flinches, and looks around for people nearby who may have heard it. But he is definitely alone.

Alagur cuts off the side branches and leaves, leaving the branch as a straight wooden pole. Alagur smiles at his handiwork.

One less slap from Edgryn if he sees I paid attention to what he was instructing us about weaponry…

Alagur smiles for a moment, but then the smile fades when he realises he faces a worse fate if he's back in the city.

CHAPTER THREE

Alagur slowly climbs up yet another hill. It seems to him the number of hills separating him from his goal of reaching Northern Blades just increases every step he takes. Darkness has set in hours earlier, and now Alagur's caution is aimed towards the animals that might come out at night to scavenge, and where he steps onto his feet. The dark of the woodland surrounds him…

Alagur stops his forward motion when he hears a sound. He hears a snarl, then another. He recognises these snarls.

"Ailep hounds," he grunts under his breath.

He listens closely. The sounds come from the south, and it means the packs of ailep hounds, which usually only traverse the landscape much further south-east of City of Wolves, were bolder, and venture closer to the regions occupied by wolves. He knows from the retellings told that the North Blades and the Upper Planes to the northeast where the wolves are located, well most of them.

But Alagur's focus is on the wolves akin to the retelling Elder Man Vaymaz has described.

He hears a loud squeal and realises the ailep hounds have been tracking a beast of some sort, and not, as his mind tries to convince him, a boy who should have been inside the massive ruined city that lies a half day away to his east.

I think I need to be cautious tonight. Those ailep hounds could easily come my way.

He looks up at the trees. He needs some rest, and the best place to avoid becoming the next meal for the beasts is to sleep many paces above the ground, then he sees a tree that may be useful…

Alagur hoists himself onto the lowest thick branch, then pulls himself onto the next one up, even though it takes some effort. After climbing up three more branches, he stops for a few minutes to catch his breath. He stops and listens again to the snarls, which seem closer now. He lifts his head to judge where the wind blows from and let's go of an audible breath when he realises the beasts won't pick up his scent.

He climbs up three further branches and finds a large hollow in the bark suitable to his need for a place to rest and perhaps sleep. He climbs inside it and places his knapsack opposite of him, and leans the makeshift spear in the small dip he sees in the bark. He's able to view the dark landscape from this vantage point and assumes that the lights far to the east are those of City of Wolves. He squints his eyes and decides the lights to the southwest come from the city he was told about recently, a place called Ruh'nar. The person who told him is *Samur…*

Alagur wonders for a few minutes what life was like inside that city, but then decides the wolf is more important. He wonders what the wolves like the legendary Mountain Ghost are really like.

Although it isn't the proper name, I think I'll call the one I get, Yalla. It almost means Mountain Ghost, if I remember my original dialect correctly. One day, I'd want to know if the retelling I heard about Mountain Ghost is the proper retelling. Something tells me Vaymaz only told the parts that matter to the Wolf Riders…

He glances back towards the distant lights of City of Wolves, wondering if he is missed already. He glances around the edge of the knotted bark towards the north. That's his next destination. He needs to reach it as fast as he can.

The longer he's missing from City of Wolves, the more chance there's that he'd be punished, and they might also take the wolf he gets for himself, and regardless of whether he bonded with it, from what he knows, the wolf could be set against him if the Wolf Masters of the city so willed it…

Most nights Samur, who declares the young Alagur as a brother, is too drunk to notice where the boy is. Alagur guesses tonight will not differ from any other. Most nights when this happens, Samur would turn up drunk at the lodgings he has at the west side of the city, and where he'd occasionally be sleeping unless he's too tired, and goes to the sleeping house he's assigned to instead. He isn't sure why Samur specifically wants him in that sleeping house.

Alagur notices that Samur snatched almost every boy or by those closest to him and therefore considered the most loyal in Samur's eyes…

Alagur decides then it's best to leave before the first light rises over the eastern skyline. He looks up at the sky above and watches the stars. He knows somewhere west is a sister possibly doing the same. He can almost remember her face, like the way she looked on that last day when he was still home.

I hope she's alright.

He can't remember her name, but always sees her young panicked face whenever he's on the edge of sleep.

Another thought enters Alagur's mind. Something about what's going on in the City of Wolves bothers him. It's almost like everything there is wrong, and another reality of people living there in peace, working there in peace, should happen instead. Unlike most boys there, he possesses some curiosity, although most days he tries to hide this curiosity from everyone, including himself.

Alagur leans back.

He's tired and sleep doesn't find him. He closes his eyes for a while, but each time an animal makes some sound, he's fully awake again. He glances down and listens to see if he senses the direction the sounds come from, but he's in a small copse, and therefore many night animals are drowning out the sounds of the specific animals, the earlier ailep hounds, that he wants to know their whereabouts of…

He doesn't hear the ailep hounds, and Alagur vows to check for anything that may show what direction they have gone.

He needs to be ready for a confrontation with them, and he's certain it wouldn't be the first or the last…

CHAPTER FOUR

Alagur wakes abruptly as the weather has turned from the warm weather of the previous day to windy weather, and it also rains. He curses under his breath when the wind pummels him with rain. He straightens up and looks around. He can't see any specific feature of City of Wolves in this weather. He feels annoyed about the weather. It will make the journey even harder, and he risks getting ill too. But the likelihood of the Wolf Riders riding out in this weather to come to find him has also become greater…

Alagur climbs down from the tree. With a soft thud, he lands on the moist forest floor. Alagur masks his scent from being picked up by the ailep hounds. He has heard men in City of Wolves talk of a method. From what they described, it's also a method which will mask him from being discovered by the wolves those same men ride. He lifts his nose, so the distinct smell he searches for can enter his nostrils.

After perhaps moving twenty paces from his original position, though doing it cautiously, he catches the distinct smell of vole droppings.

He waits for several minutes before he walks west. It isn't the direction of where the wolves are, but it has to do for now. He searches in the nearby undergrowth, where he thinks the smell comes from. When he finds the vole droppings, the stench makes Alagur's stomach churn, and he almost throws up.

That stinks as bad as always…

He bends over to scoop up the somewhat slimy substance into a piece of leather he'd pulled from his knapsack. He needs to find a place where he can mix it with ash and some of his drinking water. He's glad he prepared so well in that regard before leaving. Alagur mixes the vole droppings with the other ingredients he prepared, then applies it to his clothing and the parts of his body, which can give off an odour that wolves can smell. He knows he stinks, but with no one else around, it doesn't really matter. Alagur glances around to make sure there are no Wolf Riders near him, who may have been watching his activities all this time.

But the landscape seems devoid of any form of life form, and now Alagur notices how eerily quiet it is and he frowns. Now a nagging feeling of doubt rises in his mind about whether he's doing the correct thing; if it will be worth it. He knows he can't go back to the City of Wolves. Not now. Not without a decent wolf under his control…

He tries to determine how he might be from the wolves; he isn't entirely sure of their location. He hopes he goes in the correct direction. Alagur walks briskly. He's always loved to walk and run too. Now, speed is of the essence. It's already the middle of the day, and he sees the distant peaks of what he thinks is the Northern Blades, and realises he's no closer now than he was perhaps a day earlier. And with every step he takes, makes it seems the mountain range is even further away. He tries to recall what Elder Man Vaymaz said in the stories he told.

He said something about a valley. I'm certain of it…

He looks around. He sees the trail of what might be a lake of some sort, with a large woodland north of it. Even from this distance, Alagur can see the trees in the woodland are massive. Vaymaz didn't exaggerate about the forest. The trees are tall and seem ancient to Alagur. In his boyish mind, the forest grows even bigger than it is.

"I'm certain he mentioned woodland…" Alagur mumbles.

He walks, this time in a northwest direction. Ahead of him, trees loom on the horizon, and Alagur realises he's never seen trees this tall. He stops to look at the trees for a while. Then he looks at the lake to the south of it, which seems to stretch as far as his eyes can see. He'd heard rumours of the city on the other side of that lake, and wonders if he can visit it before getting the wolf, but then decides against it.

Alagur makes a sharp turn north. He glances at the lake once more, then sets off at a sprint to reach the woodland as fast as he's able. He increases speed the closer he gets to the woodland. Although he's only at the further eastern edge of it. When he enters the woodland, the serenity of the place soothes Alagur's mind. He decides this is a place he can return to often and vows to make sure it will happen. He walks a while, then arrives at the ravine with an enormous tree trunk leaning over it.

It has broken off at the base of the trunk, rather than being sheared off by the hands of men. The black colour of the breach in the trunk glistened in the low light of the forest, and it seems to Alagur to appear almost like the tree has become covered in tiny black gems. He runs his hand over the surface, wondering how long ago it happened, and how. Alagur pulls on one branch. It bends for a considerable bit before breaking.

It means the old tree trunk has a large quantity of moisture in it, despite lying on its side and rotting away ever so slowly.

It intrigues Alagur, an at an age where he might have been exploring options for a trade to learn as an apprentice. He, instead, uses that exploratory and often inquisitive mind to understand the world around him better. He doesn't know it yet, but one day these skills learnt will serve him in another capacity, and for an entirely different reason…

Tentatively, Alagur steps forward once he's climbed the massive tree trunk. The ravine it spans is hundreds of paces long in either direction, and it seems to Alagur it's the only way to get to the northern side of the ancient forest.

Once, long ago, the ravine he passes over so carefully was a river that ran through the northern landscape all the way from the western peaks of Northern Blades to a lake east of City of Wolves.

But long ago this river, and many others like it, dried out and became empty scars in the landscape instead…

CHAPTER FIVE

Alagur stops walking when he hears animals in the distance. His hand tightens around the makeshift spear he carved earlier in the day, and he waits for the sounds to make themselves heard again.

I wonder what that animal is.

He feels nervous now. He's deep within Venrasia Woods, which is where he's right now without realising it. There will be none to assist him here if he ends up in trouble. Alagur climbs down from the tree trunk and lets out a sigh when his feet feel the spongy forest floor underfoot. He isn't afraid of heights, but the trunk gives somewhat while he walks over it step by step; the drop below is at least the height of some of the tallest houses still standing in City of Wolves, and Alagur is certain he won't survive the fall if the tree trunk snaps in two under his weight. He looks back at the tree trunk, and on this side, it's obvious that a landslide of mud has buried the upper part of the tree. The ancient mud that did this turned to stone in the intervening thousands of years, and a layer of moss grew over it. Alagur knows the moss.

It's the type used to create moss ash, which he used in his vole dropping mixture to disguise his scent from animals, and in particular, the wolves accompanying Wolf Riders.

He stops again when the sounds are closer. Alagur looks for a place to hide that is not at ground level and decides the best option is to climb back onto the tree trunk.

Once on top of it, he waits for the animals to arrive, and doesn't need to wait long until three snarling ailep hounds lope towards him, stop to smell the air, then amaze Alagur because they walk off.

Seems my disguise works on them too…

Alagur grins. He climbs back down, though cautiously, just in case the ailep hounds come back; he isn't sure if he'll be able to defend against three of the animals when he's still untested to defend against one animal. He looks at the makeshift spear and wonders if he still needs it. The disguise keeps him from being detected even by the normal carnivorous animals in the wild. Perhaps, he can keep the spear for another day or so, to aide him in the journey, then dispose of it before he gets to where the wolves are…

Perhaps search for another nest, so I can use more vole droppings for this stinky disguise.

Alagur smirks at the thought that most boys in City of Wolves will avoid him smelling like this. He walks north, though at a slow, cautious pace. Alagur looks in all directions as he walks. He feels like he's being watched now, but by what or who isn't clear. It's a feeling that had steadily grown in the last couple of days. He'll know at a later part of his life what these sensations mean, and why he's getting them. But it makes him nervous and unsettled.

Darkness seems to come much sooner this far north in Keldarra, and especially in a dark woodland such as this.

Alagur's stomach also indicates that he'd not eaten food for two days now.

I should have tried to kill one of those ailep hounds.

Alagur feels angry now at his own inadequacies as a skilled hunter. He looks for edible mosses and mushrooms, he can cook into a vegetative stew of some sort. If he mixes in some of his salt, it can be eaten, although the taste will be very bitter. It has to do for now.

"I need to learn to hunt, and to cook as well, so I can get my own food when I'm back in the city…" Alagur mumbles. He jerks up when his voice echoes through the forest; he listens. The sound of his voice could easily attract an inquisitive animal. The animal can easily be a carnivore after its next kill. But it sets his mind racing.

Perhaps I can use that to my advantage to lure a beast to me…

He kneels down and glances around. He makes a soft murmuring sound. After a few minutes, he stops making the sound, then listens. He repeats the sound. He hears a small animal, which he thinks to be a small bovine-like creature, makes a similar sound to its offspring. He doesn't know if they live in the forest or venture into there, but if one animal makes such a sound, then more animals should do similarly. His hand grips tighter around the spear which he slowly lifts in a position in which he can either throw at an animal from some distance or thrust it into an animal's flank if it's closer to him.

Both depend on the strength of his arm, and although he'll be well-muscled by the time he has a wolf for a year, this isn't yet the case now, because he's still a boy, and although he's grown taller faster in the last two years, he's still shorter and more slightly built than most others in the city.

Alagur hears the sound of an animal scurrying around in the brush to his left. He raises to his feet and waits. He repeats the sounds the animal makes, and a moment later a very young vole appears in the clearing. Alagur aims the spear and throws it as fast as possible. It hits its mark, and although fatally wounded the squealing vole tries to rush off into the undergrowth but is not fast enough for a determined boy who sees his evening meal escaping.

Alagur grabs the beast's hind leg, then uses a fist to knock the vole unconscious. He pulls the spear from the wound, and plunges it again in the body, then repeats it.

All life ebbs from the tiny animal's body a moment later, and Alagur holds the limp vole up by one hind leg.

I guess this will have to do…

He knows there are men in the City of Wolves who eat vole meat roasted over a furious fire. He has never tasted it, so this is going to be a fresh experience for him.

Alagur wonders about how to prepare the animal for roasting then recalls seeing men just throw voles, skin and all, onto a blazing campfire.

He can do the same…

CHAPTER SIX

Alagur tugs at the vole which lies roasting on the campfire and wonders how long to roast the meat for.

I guess I'll give myself an upside down belly if it's undercooked. I guess I must try it…

Alagur pokes at the carcass, which appears very black from the recent fire and the ash coating it. He grabs an old piece of leather in his knapsack and spreads it on the ground. Using his spear end, he lifts the meat on the piece of leather, then takes out the small knife he took from one of Samur's packs when the man didn't look.

The man's wolf, Uzo, looks at the boy when Alagur does this, and almost makes him laugh when he tilts his head sideways in a *"What are you doing?"* motion. Uzo is the wolf Samur got for himself on a few months ago, and it's a black beast with dark yellow eyes, and to Alagur wolf always seems to look scruffy. He decides whatever wolf he gets, it will be well-brushed daily, unlike Uzo, who are often neglected by Samur for reasons unclear to Alagur as young as he is. The man constantly drinks alcohol, and because of that is less attuned to his surroundings than most around him.

Alagur turns the vole carcass on its back and slits the beast's belly in two like he has seen Wolf Riders who eat vole do. As soon as the slit is made, Alagur pushes the carcass away from him, so any uncooked entrails can spill out. They do and land on the ground just beyond the edge of the leather sheet. Alagur gets up and positions his seating area somewhat away from where he was preparing the vole. Once all entrails have spilt out, he grabs the leather sheet by the corners and pulls it away from where the entrails pile lies on the ground. Alagur cuts the two parts connecting it to the body, then uses a foot to push the pile further away. He pushes soil over the entrails to half-bury them. He lifts the carcass back onto the fire, now with the open belly down so that the heat of the fire would penetrate the innards of the beast, and finish the cooking process.

Alagur will eat in another hour, so uses the time he has to reorganise his knapsack. He pulls the bag on his lap and removes its content carefully. A piece of mouldy bread, found min the bottom of the bag, gets thrown toward the entrails pile. A shirt that has become spoilt because of it is thrown into the campfire as fuel. He checks every item he possesses for damage or spoilage, and he threw about half the items for fuel on the campfire and repacks the other half. When he thinks the task is done, he puts the knapsack behind him, then checks the carcase again. It seems ready…

Alagur cuts a large piece of rump from the carcass, and initially tentatively bites into it. He's surprised when it tastes better than expected. It has a rich flavour, possibly caused by the cooking process.

I can get to like this…

Alagur stamps the fire out before setting off north again. He doesn't wait to see if any animal will come to taste from the spoils of his effort. He knows the entrails will feed the scavengers that come out at night, and by morning they'll have eaten all edible items he left behind. He also leaves the leather sheet behind, now it's spoilt by blood.

Alagur walks for several hours before he sees a tree with a hollow in it. He climbs up to the hollow, and once inside it feels like this place can be a place to catch up on the lost sleep of the last several days. The silence of that night causes Alagur to fall asleep much faster, and the following morning he awakes just after sunrise. After climbing down from the tree, Alagur finds a stream to bathe.

I'm certain that any wolves won't bond with me if I stink of vole droppings.

He walks northeast and finds a small waterfall. He puts the knapsack on the ground and doesn't even undressed to get under the fast stream of what turns out to be rather chilly meltwater being fed further north by melting ice. Alagur doesn't mind it, and he stands under that stream for a considerable time, until he's certain all smell is gone.

He climbs from the stream, and sits down in the sun on a small bolder to dry himself, and gets his belly filled with some more of the cooked vole meat, which he'd butchered before he continued his travel the previous day. He looks around, then notices the field just northeast of him, filled with green and brown vegetation, and wonders if that's the dotted field from the retelling, because if, then he knows now he has to travel directly north-west for five more days and then he'd be at South Valley of Miza.

Alagur tries to recall what else Elder Man Vaymaz said about the region *where* the wolves are located. In the retelling, Vaymaz told, they live on the lower slopes of Northern Blades. He might be weeks away from where them, or just days. Only time will tell if former or latter is true…

When he has travelled another day seeing no wolves, Alagur gets worried he may be too far east for them. But he persevered…

He travels a few more days, then stops, and wait for luck to be on his side instead.

CHAPTER SEVEN

A howl wakes Alagur, and he jerks up and looks around.

Where did it come from?

Another howl… closer this time. Alagur is on his feet in seconds. He pulls his shirt on, grabs the knapsack, and places it on his back, and fastens it in place, while he listens for more of the howls. If more howls break the morning silence, a pack of wolves is close. He meanders in a northern direction. He can feel a chill in the air, which means he's getting closer to the cold Northern Blades.

Alagur pulls on his extra shirt, then sets off at a pace to warm up. He halts when he hears another howl, and it's closer now, and directly to his west. Alagur scans the landscape for movement. He sees a copse to the southwest of him, with a large section of undergrowth north of it. He can see it's further than it seems, as the landscape falls away into a shallow valley there. But he knows the sound of wolf song is coming from there…

Now walking cautiously, Alagur makes his way to the undergrowth, and when he gets there, he sees movement north of it.

He looks around then spots the wolves. Alagur is in awe of the five wolves he sees. He watches them tend to younger wolves; then Alagur sees the wolf he's hoping for.

"Yalla."

As he speaks the wolf's name, Alagur feels some surprise when the wolf lifts its head and turns to look directly at him. Their eyes lock, and Alagur smiles when he sees the wolf's beautiful golden eyes, and despite the young age, the wolf seems to be, they're already filled with unfathomable wisdom.

"Yalla…" Alagur repeats.

More of the wolves look up, and for a moment Alagur's mind wonders if they see him as their prey. The young wolf who seems to be somewhat smaller than the others, surrounding it, snorts a few times and seems to make sense of sensations it feels. The coat of the wolf is like what Elder Man Vaymaz has attributed to the ancient famous wolf he'd named *Mountain Ghost* in his stories - the wolf of the *first* Wolf Master.

Alagur looks up for a moment. Somewhere in the tall peaks beyond, where the wolves stride around, is where the famous event took place, and from where that man emerged riding his wolf. Looking back at the wolf, that he, Alagur, wants, it's obvious that initially, he'd have to walk beside the beast. Alagur smiles because it will be a compromise for the return journey.

And when he arrives back, it will clear to them that this wolf is his.

I bet they'll treat me like a returning hero…

He hopes it to be true.

The wolves flank the runt who's curious about the boy in the undergrowth. The boy inadvertently started the bonding process when he recognised this animal as potentially being a distant offspring of the original Mountain Ghost. Or, at least, related in a way through breeding.

The wolves move closer, and Alagur is uncertain for a moment if it means to happen during bonding.

Alagur straightens up.

He knows he has to approach the wolf showing no fear, and without taking his eyes off the others. He heard the men of City of Wolves speak about this. They stated a wolf who accepts a man as its equal, will give a signal to its pack the man is *one* with that pack.

It means the wolf pack around him will treat him like he's a wolf, like themselves. He watches every move they make, and as he does this, he slowly walks forward towards the wolf he calls *Yalla* already.

This wolf, Yalla, will be his own Mountain Ghost.

Alagur already imagines going into battle, riding on this wolf, and becoming a victorious hero of some sort. He knows the opposite can be true too. That he might return to City of Wolves, be treated like a disobedient boy, and be thrown in the pit with wild wolves. He already has seen Wolf Riders returning to the city who was killed in a battle, some of whom were only perhaps a year past Second Rites.

This makes it obvious *why* there's a need to snatch boys from the cities; why he ended up in the City of Wolves. Alagur audibly curses at the thought that three years earlier he was in a house with two parents and a sister he adores. It's his own stubborn foolishness that got him here.

I doubt I can reach home, so I might as well go back with the wolf and hope for the best...

Alagur waits to see what will happen. He might have preferred one of the adult wolves, but he knows the bonding process is so much easier, apparently, with the younger wolves. He glances at the wolf he'd called Yalla and suddenly finds himself drawn to *this* wolf. With good feeding, good treatment, good exercise, and plenty of patience, he might end up with a wolf that is as big, if not bigger, than the wolves flanking what seems to be the runt.

Yes, you'll be Mountain Ghost's child...

He smiles at the idea that nutritious food and care can grow the wolf into one of the biggest ones in the City of Wolves. It will be what will give him so much prestige, it can allow him to climb the ranks, and perhaps be one of those Elder Men himself one day.

Now comes the hard part. Mulling over the process of what's involved in bonding is the straightforward part. The tough part is getting it done. Alagur has watched and laughed at boys who are told to do what he's about to do. And he then teased such boys and call them *runt*, like the Wolf Riders around him did. He doesn't realise that in fact, he's a bully and that one day he'll regret the actions, and will want to say sorry to those he did this to…

Alagur stares at the wolf who'd caught his attention. A silver-grey-and-white wolf with dark golden yellow eyes. The small wolf, almost still a pup, looks up at the boy… and Alagur looks back at the wolf with a delighted smile on his face…

CHAPTER EIGHT

Alagur stares into the young wolf's eyes. Two giant yellow eyes stare back at him. The wolf lets out a yip, which makes Alagur smile. He realises a moment later the wolf is female…

"Yalla," he says softly. The wolf yips again, almost like she recognises her new name.

Have I bonded with you properly?

Alagur knows there's only one way to know. They're still in the territory of the wolf pack. He gets up and looks around for a moment. Eleven wolves all stare back at him silently. He knows the outcome of the next action. If the new wolf companion follows him, she bonded with him, and these wolves will go because they won't class his wolf as part of their pack any longer. If the wolf at his feet turns and runs back to the pack, then Alagur needs to find another pack to repeat this process. Alagur turns, and after a brief hesitation, walks away from the young wolf. Alagur holds his breath and doesn't dare to turn to look. A bonding can't be completed if he gives any verbal commands. It's nature that dictates her will here. If she decides the bond is appropriate, the wolf will follow. If she found the boy unworthy, the wolf will turn and run away.

After walking about a hundred sixty paces, Alagur stops and waits for a few minutes. He almost jumps when a sharp, audible yip comes from beside him, startling him into the realisation that he's successful with the bonding. This is an unexpected surprise for him.

"Yalla," he says again, now louder. The wolf yips a few times, then he lets out a long, eerily beautiful wolf song that sends chills down Alagur's spine. It's answered by one, then two more, wolf songs which seem distant.

Alagur turns just in time to see the alpha female of the pack disappearing into the early fog of the lower parts of the mountain, allowing the boy to understand somewhat where the ancient name for the legendary Mountain Ghost came from…

He bends down, and takes the young wolf's head in two hands, and places his forehead against the wolf's forehead.

"I'm not really allowed to name you Yalla until the Wolf Naming Ceremony, and I can't take part in one until I am due for Second Rites," Alagur says softly to the wolf, assuming that the wolf understands the meaning of his words.

Alagur scratches the wolf behind its ear and laughs when the wolf snorts. "Did that tickle you?"

He repeats the motions, and grins broadly when the wolf snorts again, and then again.

"I think we need to *go* now. I can't ride you yet, but with you, by my side, the journey will be faster, because all the ailep hounds will stay away from me."

Yalla lifts her head, bends it down to the ground, then lifts her head back up, and looks directly at her new master with golden eyes filled with newfound wisdom - a side effect of the bonding process.

Alagur has seen the same motion in wolves in City of Wolves during successful bondings. This wolf is definitely bonded to him. He knows now what the process is like for the boy in question, and why those who succeeded in it, feels like the entire world revolved around them.

Now, he's one of those boys. But only he knows that. He needs to go back to show off the wolf. On the way he can kill as much as he can, to allow the wolf to eat well and grow strong. It will be just a few weeks anyway before the wolf will reach to waist height, and by the end of next season, the wolf will be as tall as the others Alagur has seen in the city. He also realises he needs to teach signals to the wolf. He knows Wolf Riders have two types.

They use a range of whistles, but also hand motions are used, and Alagur realises he doesn't know what the hand motions might mean. He also remembers seeing that different Wolf Riders have different hand motions, and guesses from this they're unique to each man.

"Let's go," Alagur says, and he motions with his hand. He walks, then stops, and sees the wolf still standing in one place. He frowns, and for a moment wonders if he's wrong to think he'd bonded with the wolf. He looks at the wolf a moment, then repeats the command and hand gesture, and then just walks, assuming the wolf will follow. She does, though not immediately.

It's an hour later when Alagur finally realises the wolf isn't only following him, but also now expects where he might go next. Alagur makes a game of it. Alagur changes the direction he walks. The wolf is confused at first, then follows. Alagur changes direction, and this time the wolf expects the alteration.

A hand signal; the wolf stops walking. Another one and the wolf rushes to the boy, almost knocking him over. He laughs out loud.

"I think you and I *will* be friends for a long time," Alagur says as he scratches the wolf behind its ears once more, then he thinks, *Yes, we will…*

Alagur thinks of a hand gesture he can do to allow the wolf to attack whoever or whatever he wants. If he can teach it well enough, his arrival at the city will be safer, but only as long as they don't throw him in the pit of wolves the moment he steps through the gatehouse on the western side of the city. He knows he's already been away for ten days, and if he's away for almost double that, he'll be in serious trouble arriving back there.

I need to learn to ride you sooner.

Alagur looks at the animal beside him. If he rides the wolf now, his feet will drag over the ground. But he needs to try…

Alagur holds the wolf by its scruff. He murmurs soothing words under his breath. Slowly, he slides his left leg over the top of the wolf and then straightens up. It surprises the wolf for a moment, then tries to reach back to nip Alagur's leg. Alagur moves his leg back. That causes the wolf to try for the other leg. When she fails with that, she shakes herself, and a moment later Alagur lies flat on his back on the ground, with Yalla leaning over him growling a bit.

Alagur isn't angry. He thinks of it as funny. "I guess you're just as stubborn as I am..." he exclaims.

The wolf snorts as if to show she disproves his assessment of her...

CHAPTER NINE

Alagur lifts himself to an upright position, then looks at the wolf who now sits on her hind legs, and tilts her head sideways, like she feels curious about the whole situation. He smiles at the wolf.

"I guess we need to *try* that exercise again…"

Alagur gets up and walks to the wolf. He scratches the wolf's ears and murmurs at her. Then turns and walks away. When he turns, he sees the wolf heeled him. He scratches the wolf's ears again, then takes hold of the scruff once more, and glancing down at the wolf a moment, he slides his left leg once more over the back of the wolf, then straightened himself on her back.

He waits, expecting a nip to come once again, but the wolf buckles, and pushes the boy off her back so he lands on the ground in a seated position… *this* time. Yalla turns and looks at the boy with what Alagur can only describe as a 'wolf's grin'. The wolf is playing a game of her own at his expense and getting a delight out of it.

"Right, now you're going to let me on your back… YALLA," Alagur says forcefully as he gets up again, and he puts emphasis on the wolf's name.

Once he's upright, again he just scratches the wolf's ears, and murmurs at her. He's seen Wolf Riders, including Samur, beat their wolves into submission. He doesn't want that. He wants this wolf to be his true loyal companion, like Mountain Ghost was to the first Wolf Master. It means he has to find the patience to get the wolf to allow him on her back unhindered. Even if this takes him all day, and then some more days.

I'm doing it wrong I guess…

Alagur looks at the wolf. He saunters to the left side of the wolf.

He stops and looks again at the wolf.

"Are you going to let me ride you?"

The wolf yips and shows her wolf's grin again.

"I guess you're teasing me to teach me something…"

The wolf answers by licking his face. Alagur brushes off the moist. It just causes the wolf to repeat it.

"Alright, so you get to lick my face, and I'm not allowed to ride you. Is that it?"

Alagur's eyes fly open when the wolf turns ninety degrees and stands to look at him. Alagur doesn't wait. He takes hold of the scruff, and lifts his left leg over, tentatively at first, then fully.

A moment later, he lifts himself on top of the wolf. He sits there waiting for the bolt to knock him off again, but opens his mouth in amazement when the wolf moves forward. Yalla walks a few steps, then stops. Alagur is about to wonder if that's the end of it when suddenly the wolf sets off at a high speed in an almost southern direction. Alagur leans forward and wraps his arms around the wolf's neck, which he can feel rippling under his arms. The wind bites into his face and the dew in the air becomes a blanket of mist causing his hair to turn into wet strands, but despite it, Alagur has a big grin on his face from the excitement he feels now.

After about ten minutes, the wolf slows to a slow pace, but never really stops moving, and then Alagur notices the wolf instinctively turns southeast and the direction where, a few days from their current location, is the City of Wolves…

Slowly Alagur pulls himself up into an upright position, always cautious of his motions, just in case the wolf bolts him off again.

Finally, after another half hour, the wolf stops completely. She twists her body, so she glances back at Alagur. He gets the idea she tells him, *"You can get off me now"*

Alagur slides off the wolf's back and slumps down on the

ground. The ride was fun, but it's tiring, too.

I guess we can try another ride tomorrow…

Alagur wipes over his forehead and hair to wipe away the mist that settled there. He has ridden on this wolf, when many boys in City of Wolves are unsuccessful for weeks or even months. Although at first unsuccessful, he'd done it after a few attempts.

And Alagur hopes it isn't fluke…

He gets up and looks to see where he is. He's surprised when he realises they're almost halfway to the massive ancient forest, and that they did the distance in about a day of riding when on foot it took him three days to do the same distance.

I'll be back in the City of Wolves in about a week at this pace.

Alagur smiles at the thought the travel is so much faster with a wolf rather than without one. But then, the realisation sets in, that in seven days from now, he might be severely punished for running off to get a wolf. The wolf seems to sense a change in Alagur's mood, and walks closer to the boy, and stops beside the boy flanking him from the right. It gives Alagur a sense of comfort, and he puts his arm around the neck of the wolf. The wolf nudges the boy gently, and although Alagur's mood is now sombre, he manages a smile for a few fleeting moments.

Alagur takes hold of the scruff, then slides a leg over the wolf. A moment later, he sits on the wolf and it surprises him that, this time, the motion is effortless. He pushes the wolf's neck muscle on the right and pulls gently on the wolf's scruff on the left.

"We need to go to a massive city filled with other wolves…"

It seems the wolf understands the motions because she sets to a gentle pace towards the south-east, neither going too fast nor too slow. This time Alagur sits on the wolf in an upright position and feels awe that he now rides the beast properly.

I guess I must learn to make a saddle and a harness for you…

Slowly, the journey takes him closer to City of Wolves, but what fate awaits him there, he's still uncertain of…

CHAPTER TEN

Alagur glances over his shoulder. He drives the wolf into the undergrowth when he catches sight of a group of men riding their wolves. The distance between them and him prevents him to see who they are, but he's certain this will happen more and more the closer he gets to the city that now is visible on the horizon. There are perhaps only another two days riding before he'd be there, and the assessment it might take about seven days to return was correct.

Alagur climbs off Yalla's back, she snorts softly, and he lies his hand over her nose bridge to calm her.

"Shh, they'll hear you," he whispers.

Alagur puts his arm around the neck of the wolf. He can feel her hairs stand up.

"They're not an enemy," Alagur whispers. "I just don't want to be seen arriving…"

He scratches Yalla's ear to calm her. The soft undercurrent of growling coming from her throat lessens, and after a time her hair stops standing up.

Alagur watches the group of men.

He's uncertain who these men are, but he can tell they're on some sort of hunting forage, based on the number of dead carcasses hanging from bindings from several of the wolves. He's glad now he rubbed the last of his vole mixture on Yalla, so these wolves won't catch her scent so easily. It will be to his disadvantage if these men discover him and Yalla, so Alagur decides to wait for their departure. After what seems half the day, the men finally leave, and by the time they do, they're drunk, and Alagur can smell the stench of alcohol in the light easterly breeze.

"Come…" he motions the wolf with the hand signal he's been teaching her over the last few days.

He walks without waiting to see if the wolf will follow, but the warm body temperature of the wolf he senses close to his left, tells Alagur she follows him closely. It's one command he'd taught her. All the others will come over the years to come if he survived his arrival back in the city.

Alagur looks around constantly for other Wolf Riders who may also be on a hunting forage. But the landscape is empty.

Evidence in this landscape shows that once, in a distant past, it was a beautiful, tranquil and very luscious landscape, but the Wolf Riders occupying the City of Wolves for perhaps the last thousand years or more, aren't known for a skill of farming or husbandry. They're warriors who terrorise the land Keldarra with thieving, pillage and snatching of young, unsuspecting boys.

Alagur wonders for a moment how the landscape might look if instead the city may thrive in its original state. This assessment of the situation in the city is already setting Alagur apart from the other boys, who are snatched either before or after him, or as he. And this view of the world will grow and ultimately lead to a new normal for him, which will set in motion later events he doesn't know about yet…

Alagur sees movement in the distance and quickly dives into nearby undergrowth. The wolf follows the boy with no hesitation. Alagur feels grateful for her presence suddenly. He watches the man walk past. It isn't a Wolf Rider, but a simple merchant, travelling apparently from the east towards the lake Alagur had seen days earlier. The man is in his mid-thirties and is unaware he's so close to the danger of City of Wolves and blissfully unaware that the eyes of a young boy, and those of a young wolf, both look at him with great interest.

After he's alone once more, Alagur travels for the next hour by staying under the cover of the undergrowth.

Alagur stops walking when it becomes apparent the

undergrowth thins, and he spends the rest of the day and that night there. Tomorrow he'll be in the city, and he needs to be well-rested and alert for whatever may happen. He sleeps, curled up against the chest of Yalla, who whimpers occasionally to get him to play with her as he did on previous nights.

But a sullen mood overtakes the boy's mind, and for most of the night, he lies awake thinking about what to say about his absence, or what to do if they try to take the wolf from him. He's uncertain how he will react if Wolf Riders meant to kill Yalla…

He wakes before sunrise, having fallen asleep eventually from the warmth Yalla's body generates. Alagur eats the last of the dried meat suited for his own consumption, then dumps all the food on the ground, and lets Yalla take her pick off the morsels until her belly is filled sufficiently. He gets up, then straps the knapsack on his back, and practises the latest command with Yalla once more. If trouble comes, he wants to be sure she'll defend him with her life.

Alagur sees Yalla's stance stiffen to a defence posture, and she sniffs the air as she searches it for the smell of whatever he wants her to attack. He gives another signal, and the stance softens back to her almost playful pup-like pose.

"I think that'll have to do," Alagur says softly as he scratches behind the wolf's ear to show affection and approval of her behaviour.

She snorts, and Alagur smiles, but decides the sound of him laughing loud this close to the city might attract the wrong attention. If he goes back into the city, it will be through stealth.

"We've to go in silently," he says to the wolf, "Can you be silent?"

Yalla shakes her head in an up-down motion like she was saying, *"Yes, I can…"*.

Alagur walks to her left flank, pulls his leg over her body, and climbs.

No protest comes from the animal. She's completely

conditioned now to the bonding, and in her own wolfish way, regards the boy as a friend, and also perhaps something like a brother in a litter. As the only surviving pup of a doomed litter, she was at the mercy of the generosity of aunts, who'd offer her some of their milk, but not enough to feed her sufficient.

When Alagur's hand feeds her with plenty, it grows the bond of loyalty she feels for the boy, and this kind act from the boy is ultimately what wins her to his side, so he can call himself Wolf Rider…

CHAPTER ELEVEN

A massive hand strikes across Alagur's face as he turns the corner. Edgryn sneers at him. "So where have you been?" he asks angrily, almost screaming every syllable of the sentence.

Alagur flashes an angry stare at the tall man, then he hears the wolf, standing a few paces behind him, growling. It takes Edgryn a few minutes to realise the boy isn't alone, and that he, in fact, seems to control a wolf.

"How did you get *that* wolf?" he asks, now lowering his voice, so not to invite more growling from the beast, and also to prevent it from possibly attacking him. He observes the wolf, and his keen eye notes the wolf is still mostly wild, but that it's bonded…

"You bonded with it…?" Edgryn says finally, awe clear now in his voice, but he also still sounds angry and full of disdain for the disobedient boy.

"I did," Alagur replies, and suddenly he feels he gained an advantage over this man in some inexplicable way. He glances at the wolf over his shoulder and tries one signal he'd practice. The wolf nears… *slowly*.

"You already mastered the skill of commanding a wolf… impressive…"

Alagur spins around. He looks at Vaymaz and sees a delightful smirk on the old man's face. He looks directly at Edgryn, and Alagur realises the old man finds something about the fear of Edgryn very humorous. Then he laughs loud, holding his belly, which shakes because of it. Behind the boy, Edgryn laughs too. After a few moments, Alagur can't resist joining in, and he laughs too.

"I guess you earned your place among us as Wolf Rider…"

Edgryn's voice isn't filled anymore with disdain for the boy, but he sounds like he admires the boy. Alagur smiles at the man.

"There will be much to learn still," Vaymaz says, now sounding stern instead.

Alagur nods at him.

"I tried to learn what I saw being taught," Alagur says.

"Ah, so that's *why* the wolf defends you," Edgryn says, "How long ago did you find this wolf?"

"I rode back on her. I found her seven days ago," Alagur says.

"Not many learn *that* fast," Vaymaz smiles at the boy.

"But I did," Alagur blushes suddenly because it seems to him that he spoke out of turn.

He jerks around quick to see if Edgryn is about to strike him for it, but the man stands there grinning, with both hands planted squarely on his hips, and staring at Vaymaz.

"What do you plan to do with him?" he asks the Elder Man.

This makes Alagur look back at Vaymaz, wondering what he has planned.

"I'll let fate decide that," Vaymaz says, "You take him to his sleeping house *after* you showed him where to keep this wolf. So, he knows where to get *her* when the time is right…"

Vaymaz turns and walks off, leaving both Alagur and Edgryn looking at each other with puzzled looks on their faces.

"He's always been strange and cryptic," Edgryn says. "Come, bring the wolf too, although I don't know how he knew the wolf is female…"

Alagur follows Edgryn, who walks away immediately in tall strides, and the boy signals the wolf to follow him. She does, but behind him rather than at his side. It seems the earlier distrust for the man she'd felt hasn't fully disappeared from her body, which still is in a defensive stance.

But after a few frantic hand signals, the wolf becomes relaxed again.

"She can sleep *here*," Edgryn points at an enclosure, before continuing to speak, "That there is *my* wolf, and most of these wolves belong to my squad, so they'll safeguard her. I can *see* why you went for her. She has the appearance like the one from Elder Man Vaymaz's retelling, and I'm certain you'll name her appropriately... *if* you haven't done so yet..."

Alagur nods but stays silent. He leads his wolf into the enclosure and watches as Edgryn closes the gate.

"You must catch up with your many tasks. I'll feed her myself, so don't worry about her," Edgryn says.

"Was I missed?" Alagur whispers.

"You were. But not by many. I went hunting when I noticed *you* were gone. I stayed away for twelve days. It was Vaymaz, who suggested for me to do it," Edgryn says, "Everyone thinks you went with me. Even Samur and he now scowls at me every time he sees me. I think he assumes I'm trying to lure you to my squad..."

Alagur frowns. This isn't the same Edgryn from before the journey. This Edgryn seems to be respectful of him, even seems to admire him.

"What task do I need to do...?" he asks.

"I've said to those doing the cooking for tonight's feast to expect you there. I suggest you go there," Edgryn says, "And Alagur... never ever leave the city, like you did, *again*. If you do, use it as an opportunity to stay *away*. There are... things that are dangerous *here*, which can lead to an uncertain fate. Always remember *that*. It can lead you to the pit with wild wolves faster than this wolf can run from this enclosure to the pit to save you..."

Alagur nods and swallows hard. It's a lesson he'll never forget…

Alagur runs to the cooking area, which is at the southern side of the city. Here, he's met by Belduran, who stands to speak to Rudrig and two other men. They look at him with stern expressions on their faces, but none of them speak to him. He looks at the four men as he walks into the cooking area.

"Right then, you finally got here, you lazy runt…"

Alagur jerks his head to see a man standing in his way, with a sneer on his face. In the red and orange flames of the cooking fires, the man looks even more menacing to Alagur's young mind.

"I'm here to help with the cooking," he says sheepishly and doesn't realise until the next words spoken, who the man is.

"So, I'm to hold my pack brother on a leash like a runt, so he doesn't steal from me, and run away…"

Alagur stops walking, and stares hard through the smoke, then realises the man who spoke is none other than Samur…

CHAPTER TWELVE

Alagur looks around. There are only a few boys at the location where the feast is planned. None of them are ones he knows personally…

"Alagur, come…"

Alagur looks up, feeling surprised. It's the first time the man he knows as Elder Man Belduran has spoken to him. He puts the sack of meat he carries on a nearby table and catches the glances and nudges from the other boys. He suddenly feels aware that this might be when he will get punished, but glancing at Belduran's face, it shows a calm serenity that's uncommon among most Wolf Riders.

"I think you know why you're coming with me," Belduran says.

Alagur nods.

He can guess why. He's uncertain if the guess is correct, or not.

Belduran walks at a steady pace across the vast city, followed by Alagur, who becomes more anxious with every step they take.

He feels surprised when they arrive at a building close to the enclosure where he sees Yalla get up and wag her tail in recognition. She stops wagging when Alagur keeps walking on.

They motion to Alagur to enter a building. When his eyes adjust, he sees nine men seated there. Among them are Rudrig, Vaymaz, Edgryn, Samur, and others whose names Alagur doesn't know.

"We *know* you left the city without authorisation," an Elder Man states. "We want you to explain to us *why* you did it."

"I did it because of the retelling Elder Man Vaymaz told us,"

Alagur says deciding it is no use evading the questions asked.

Every man in the room looks at Vaymaz, who appears unfazed by the sudden inclusion of himself in the reason for the boy's absence.

"Yes, I told a retelling. The retelling of Mountain Ghost," he states.

"That's just a retelling. It's nothing more than that," Samur says.

"It's based on true events," Vaymaz says, "We all know it's the retelling of the first Wolf Master…"

"That's what you believe," Samur says, "I have a different--"

"We're here to discuss the fate of this boy, not to decide whether a retelling is true, or otherwise," Belduran interjects.

Alagur feels uncomfortable while the confrontation between the various Elder Men goes on. He, like almost all other boys in the city, and even most of the Wolf Riders have seen none of them disagree so openly. He thinks Samur, who has only been an Elder Man for a season, is trying to assert a position among them.

"I think he needs to be punished for the disobedience he showed," Alagur glances for a moment at the Elder Man who spoke. It's not a man he knew, and he feels his heart beat faster with fear when he hears the words.

"I think he can *be* a Wolf Rider…" Alagur looks up sharply when he hears the words. It's Edgryn who'd spoken. Alagur sees one other staring at the man, but this man shows seething anger.

Why is Samur so angry?

It's a question to which he won't get any immediate answer. At least not until unknown events in an unknown future will take his life on an alternative path of destiny…

Alagur looks closer at Edgryn, who winks at him inconspicuously.

"I'm also convinced of that, but we need to wait until he's older," Belduran says.

Alagur looks at the Elder Man when he says this, but he worries more when Samur speaks again.

"I think the *pit* is a place for disobedience," Samur says, "Not on the back of a wolf…"

Alagur wonders why Samur of all people would say that.

"I'm surprised that *you* of all people say that," Rudrig says, "You, who never even explained *why* you joined us, is trying to deny a courageous boy his place among us…"

"Where I'm from doesn't matter. I know you, and others, are against me," Samur says.

"I agree with Samur. He needs to be taught a lesson," another Elder Men, whose name Alagur doesn't know, states.

Alagur feels scared now. He feels like any moment now one of them can just pick him up and drag him to the pit.

"Why are you all saying these things? I'm a Wolf Rider. I rode my wolf here. I can command her. She's *my* wolf," Alagur screams at the top of his voice.

All Elder Men fall silent. Some of them look angry, while others nod with knowing smiles.

"You say you rode your wolf?" Belduran asks.

"Yes, I *did*," Alagur says.

"I saw him command *his* wolf. He speaks the truth," Edgryn says.

"I saw the *same* thing," Vaymaz adds.

"Then why am I being thrown in the pit?" Alagur screams.

"Because you're disobedient," another voice answers. Alagur looks to see who speaks. It's the final unknown Elder Men who said the words.

"It seems we have an impasse here. *Half* of us agree to make you a Wolf Rider, the other half want to punish you," Belduran says, "With which group do *YOU* agree, Alagur…?"

Alagur looks at the Elder Man, is about to speak, then shuts his mouth. He opens his mouth again to say something, then closes it, and stands with an expression that's a mixture between curiosity, fear, confusion and anger on his face, and isn't able to work out what answer to give.

"Why are you asking me?" he asks in the end.

"To be a Wolf Rider is to know how to handle a difficult, unknown situation. You're in such a situation now," Belduran says, "Your wolf has it easier. She either follows your lead or selects her own will to lead her to her next actions. If she wants to be free of this situation, either she *or* you will need to be out of the equation. So, it's either in the pit for you, or you as her master until her last days. Which will you choose?"

Alagur feels confused. But he can see the outcome of the dilemma.

"What has it got to do with me choosing a group here?" Alagur asks.

"Because, if you choose one, you die," Rudrig answers, "And if you choose the other, it will be your wolf…"

"Then I choose neither," Alagur screams, "I'll let you all choose whatever fate you want for me. If I can't be *her* Wolf Rider, then she's no one's wolf, not even mine. If I can't live, then she has to die *too*…"

Alagur rushes from the building, his face streaked with tears. He feels fearful now he had firsthand experienced of one of the harshest parts of the reality of how the Wolf Riders treat one another; a reality where none cares about a young boy at all.

If I do become this Wolf Rider, as some of them suggest, I'll make sure I treat the surrounding boys in the right way when I see them.

In his frightened state, he rushes past the enclosure without even acknowledging his wolf, before he finally slumps down, and digs his head in his arms, and cries uncontrollably...

CHAPTER THIRTEEN

A shadow casts itself over Alagur, who only notices it after several minutes. He looks up to find Samur standing in front of him, making him feel even smaller.

"What will happen to me?" he asks, letting out a sob.

"Some of them want you severely punished for what you did," Samur scolds, "Others, myself included, want you as a Wolf Rider at your First Rites..."

"Can I be with the wolf?" Alagur asks.

Samur nods and pulls him onto his feet and almost drags him to the enclosure. He opens the gate, and Alagur walks inside it. Yalla rushes toward him and lies down when Alagur slumps down on the ground. Alagur watches as Samur shuts the gate.

"I'll speak to them," Samur says, "You wait here..."

Alagur frowns, but says nothing, and pulls his arm tighter around the wolf's neck. He swallows hard. He didn't realise his departure, and his arrival back would complicate things - both for himself and for others around him. He watches as Samur joins those others, whom he and others like himself, call Elder Men. They're having a heated debate, and arms pointing in his direction, show that it's about him.

Samur's gesturing is as animated as those around him, and although none of the men shout, the wind carries their louder-than-normal voices. Alagur feels a knot of worry grow. A nudge from the wolf shows the wolf is aware of his emotions.

"Don't worry, Yalla," he whispers, "They rarely kill the wolves..."

Alagur knows about the pit of wild wolves. He was threatened as often as any other boy with being thrown in it. But today the change increased so much more. He returned with a wolf, and from what the Elder Men saw, he's bonded with the wolf. The only three options open to them are; to accept the boy and wolf; to separate boy and wolf, and kill the wolf; to separate them and throw the boy into the pits. However, Samur defends the boy's actions…

"I think you caused turmoil among the Elder Men…"

Alagur looks up in surprise at Edgryn, who stands beside him, and grins at him. For once, Edgryn feels admiration, even pride, for the boy who was put in his charge to be taught the skills of being a Wolf Rider.

"I spoke with one of the other men earlier about you. He'll help me with training you *fast*. I think you're going to need it."

"Why?" Alagur asks.

"Because they're at loggerheads about whether to throw you in the pits or to let you become a Wolf Rider early," Edgryn says, "It seems you have an ally among them, perhaps *two* of them, although personally, I'd be very careful about allying yourself with Samur."

Alagur nods.

He notices the odd distrust of others towards Samur but doesn't know why this is the situation.

"They say things about him. Things that don't explain who he is, or why he's here among us," Edgryn continues, "My life is probably at risk now, because I warned you. He has his spies everywhere, and if he notices that anyone tampers with his plans, whatever they may be, he becomes angry, and then you'd best just voluntarily jump in the pit because that's a better fate than whatever he has in mind for those who stand against him…"

Alagur frowns. This is the first time Edgryn spoke to him like he's a man already. All the posturing has left the man, and when Alagur looks at the man from the corner of his eye, he sees a man who seems broken in battle.

"He'll *know that* I warned you. Just remember to always be cautious around him." Edgryn turns and walks away. Alagur stares for a while as the man walks off. It will be one of the last times he'd see him. He glances back at the group of Elder Men having heated discussion and looks at each of them to work out who Edgryn refers to. Suddenly, he realises…

He watches the man he calls a friend and perhaps brother discussing him, and gesticulating profusely, then pointing in his direction without even looking at him. He listens, and although he can't work out everything said, he catches the words 'best wolf here' and 'I have plans' coming from Samur. He wonders *why* the man cares more about his wolf than him, then shrugs off the thought.

Vaymaz, Rudrig, and even Belduran keep saying, *"No, no, no"* to whatever suggestions are being voiced by Samur. What the reason is for this denial of whatever request Samur is making is uncertain to Alagur. But it reinforces Edgryn's words to be cautious. Alagur realises he knows *who* he has to be cautious of…

After a time, Alagur sees Samur walk back towards him. The man seems to show glee on his face, like he's won a victory. But Alagur also sees him look in the direction Edgryn had walked, and when he does his best effort can't hide the disgust off his face.

"You're now in my care until Second Rites," Samur says, "I've convinced *them* it's important to get you to do your Wolf Naming Ceremony a year after your First Rites. I said I'm going to have you accompany me on campaigns after that, and I cannot have you call the wolf-like, *'Hey wolf'* and all that nonsense…"

Alagur nods.

"This enclosure isn't appropriate for the wolf. I don't think you should be in the sleeping house anymore either," Samur says, "There's a dwelling near where I live which will serve you. It has a courtyard for your wolf, and the room upstairs from it may be small, but I think it was where the rich people lived before…"

Alagur frowns for a moment, then nods. He's uncertain for the reason he's going to live there, but decides it's perhaps easier to just accept it. There isn't anything he can do about it, anyway. Not *yet*, at least…

He follows Samur across the city, followed closely by his wolf, and his wolf keeps looking behind her at the black wolf Uzo, who growls at her from time to time, asserting himself as the leader of the pack. Uzo makes Alagur feel uncomfortable now, and to him, it feels like he's being treated more like a prisoner being escorted, rather than a pack brother Samur calls him previously.

"Up there is where I live," Samur points at an alleyway beyond which Alagur can make out a stone house with a large balcony.

"And up here you'll live," Samur says.

Alagur looks around and is surprised by the spaciousness of the surrounding courtyard. To his left, he sees a stairway which seems to lead to a patio, and he can make out a house of some sort up there. Opposite of him, he sees a large dark door…

"That's where I store food and drink," Samur says, "If you want to eat, just help yourself to whatever is inside there…"

CHAPTER FOURTEEN

Alagur does his best to settle into the new reality of preparing to be a Wolf Rider. It has been several weeks since his confrontation with two dozen Elder Men, who opted to force the boy to set his own fate in motion. He caused an uproar when he countered their ultimatum with his own, which was a brave act in the eyes of several of those there. The boy's actions confirm the suspicions of some there, that their assessment of the world is correct, and they meet in private and high secrecy to discuss something else.

The question on their minds isn't, *"Will this boy be a Wolf Rider?"* but is *"Will this boy be the end as they foretold it?"*

Those who have this thought, are certain there's something more going on now beyond the ravages of the Wolf Riders causing turmoil in the world, but none of them says a word about it to others and the least of all to Alagur whose safety they now have to secure until it's time…

Alagur is oblivious of all the intrigue going on among the Elder Men, and neither he nor any of the other boys in the city are privy to that information. But he notices an alteration in Samur's behaviour after that day, and his own caution increases gradually as time goes on.

Training is hard. He's passed from Elder Man to Elder Man to learn specific skills. Alagur discoverers *why* Edgryn constructs the spears. They are what the man calls 'spear arrows', and there are apparent in *two* situations when they use them - either they throw them from a spear thrower, or with the larger ones, they're catapulted against a city being attacked. Edgryn busies himself teaching the boy the skill of using the spear thrower, and soon the boy becomes as good at the skill as his teacher.

Every day, before Alagur leaves him, Edgryn whispers his words of caution to the boy:

"Be cautious of him, Alagur. He doesn't forgive his enemies, and he doesn't forgive his friends even less. There's something about him that worries most Elder Men. He's been here just a year longer than you, and already is an Elder Man himself, when he's untested as a leader. He wants something, but no one here knows what. If something happens to me, you know I spoke the truth…"

Alagur always saunters back to his dwelling and is always fearful when he arrives there. But even fear passes over time, and Alagur soon lulls Samur's senses. He makes the man believe he's his most loyal and trusted friend. But already a plan forms itself in his mind.

A plan, based on something that happened one cold evening, when he woke up in a sweat.

I dreamt and saw a girl…

He doesn't know who she is, where she is, or why she appears in the dream. But he doesn't dwell on it when the dream is the only one, and then he gets distracted by participating in his first excursion of Wolf Riders attacking a city. He stays in the camp making weapons, while others attack. He watches the unknown city in the distance somewhat absentmindedly, while preparing the pitch for Edgryn's spear arrows.

He sees the result of the weaponry and stares fixated at the red and orange flames in the distance until Yalla beside him whimpers. The smell of pitch and the smell of burning wood drifting from the city overstimulates her nose, which is more sensitive to smells than his own.

"I'll bathe you tonight when we're back in City of Wolves," Alagur scratches the wolf behind her ears. Alagur doesn't know the name of the city. All he knew is that it lies somewhat northeast of the City of Wolves.

He scans the city outline and sees the contrast that strikes as odd.

Whereas the city seems in flames, there's a building on a high hill on the northern side of the city which seems untouched by the carnage going on around it. He knows he won't get any answers if he asks about it, so stores the knowledge away in his mind for later, so he can try to solve the puzzle by himself.

The shouts later in the evening, tell Alagur they have their success in the city, whatever it may have been. Those same men later sit around several bonfires exchanging stories, drinking ale, and shouting insults at the newly arrived boys, which send a chill up Alagur's spine when he realises that he *too* is one of them…

I have to leave.

It's the first time Alagur thinks this thought, rather than the conditioning of wanting to stay. However, as much he wants to be a Wolf Rider, something deep down inside him makes him realise leaving means more to him now.

I want to be with my parents and my sister again.

Alagur walks past each of the men with a bag containing alcohol and dodges a few blows from fists when he spills the drink. The situation is precarious. But among all the men, he notices one man who never accepts a drink from him, and who seems to drink from his own water bag. The man watches Alagur closely, and later, when almost all there are fast asleep from too much alcohol, he approaches the boy…

Alagur spins around in shock when the man speaks to him in a dialect he has almost forgotten, asking him about a city he barely remembers. After talking for about twenty minutes, the man walks off, and it leaves Alagur wondering who he is because he never said his name during the conversation. Alagur shuts his eyes for a time and tries to remember home after that conversation. He can almost remember it every time…

In the memory, he sees the little girl a few times, though she seems to fade from the memories as time goes on. He sees a room filled with large wooden vats. A man with grey hair, and himself as a small boy.

In the memory, the man tells him not to go into the streets. And he sees himself shouting back that he's going anyway…

And then the girl would run after him, calling out. *"Alagur, Alagur…"*

It's always at that moment the memory fades. And no matter what he does, Alagur cannot get any other details to show.

"Something links the memory with everything here…"

What else he wants to think about is uncertain because sleep overtakes his mind at that moment…

CHAPTER FIFTEEN

Alagur gets a rude awakening when Samur lifts him off the ground by his shirt.

"I told you to go get me some wine," Samur shouts.

He slaps his large hand across Alagur's face.

"Leave the boy alone…"

Alagur falls on the ground when Samur lets go of him, and Samur turns to face the man who spoke to him.

"Or what?" he shouts.

"Or you'll deal with me, you runt…"

It dazes Alagur. He wonders for several minutes who's speaking to Samur, then realises it's the same voice as that of the man who asked him about Chiva'na.

Why is this man defending him? Who is he?

"He needs to bring me my wine," Samur shouts, "I'm thirsty, I need a drink…"

Alagur scrambles to his feet, ducks to avoid being grabbed by Samur, and dives towards a pack where he knows there will be a wine sack.

I wonder why he calls Samur a runt… Alagur thinks as he walks back to Samur.

Alagur gets as close to Samur as he dares to go, holds the wine sack out to the man, and when Samur grabs it from his hands, he ducks again and rushes off towards his wolf to avoid Samur's angry outburst even more. He'd noted a long time ago that Samur seems fearful of the wolf, even if the man tries to claim to others around him over the campfires that one day he'll lead a squad, and all those who follow him, will end up with a wolf that's an offspring of his own wolf Uzo, and of the wolf Alagur brought back with him.

He even tries to claim that those wolves will be braver than Mountain Ghost, and a lot more fearsome.

He'll better stay away from you, or I'll cut his throat.

Alagur glares at the man while scratching behind Yalla's ears for comfort. He might be Samur's pack brother now - Samur did the ceremony at long last - but it didn't lessen the explosive, abusive behaviour he'd show. Samur leaves after a while, perhaps to go find wine at one of the other bonfires.

Alagur feels a hand on his left shoulder, and looking up, is surprised to see Edgryn knelt beside him with the other man standing behind him.

"Alagur, this man is Jymar. He's from the same place you came from originally. He wants you to go with him, to talk to him. Take your wolf with you, so she's safe," Edgryn says gently.

Alagur never heard Edgryn speak in such a gentle tone before, and frowns in confusion for a moment.

"Please come, Alagur. I want to talk with you…" Jymar says.

Alagur nods, he gets up and signals the wolf who's at his side a moment later. The skill of command over the wolf surprises Jymar, and he raises an eyebrow in admiration for the boy. He turns and walks at a fast pace towards the western side of the camp. Here he signals his own wolf to come with him. Now, to any man's eye, it may appear he's a scout who teaches a boy new skills with his wolf.

"Edgryn is a friend of mine. He told me about you when he heard you talk to your wolf," Jymar says, "He knows a few words of our dialect which I've taught him, and realised the word you spoke to your wolf, is, in fact, its name. You know it's forbidden to name your wolf before having done the Wolf Naming Ceremony…"

Alagur nods.

"I decided I needed to talk to you because we come from the same city… Chiva'na," Jymar says, "Do you remember it, Alagur?"

"Not much," Alagur says, "I've been here seven years now… I think…"

"How old were you when you came here?" Jymar asks.

"I was in my eleventh year… at least I think so," Alagur says.

"If that's the case, you can do your Wolf Naming Ceremony in another year," Jymar says, "I'll make sure you're prepared for the test they'll do during it. It seems… that Samur isn't teaching you at all. I'm uncertain why, but something tells me you're among the best here. *She* also said so…"

Alagur blushes when he heard the words of compliment, but feels perplexed at a mention of 'she' in the comment. His expression causes Jymar to laugh out loud.

"There are two others coming with us. To others, it will seem that we're teaching you the skill of scouting," Jymar says.

Alagur sees Jymar nod, and a few minutes later two men approach.

"These are my friends, Delgrun and Jervis. They're my companions… so to speak… whenever I do my scouting," Jymar says.

Alagur nods a greeting at the two men, who each smirk, then nod back. He looks at the three men for a moment, wondering if they'll be like all those who are calling themselves Samur's *friends*, but he doesn't see any malice on their faces.

"Nice wolf you have," Jervis says.

"I heard you travelled far to get her," Delgrun adds.

"I did," Alagur says, feeling shy now.

"That makes you brave. Perhaps, even braver than most of us here," Jervis says.

Alagur smiles and feels grateful for the compliment.

"Let's ride, before Samur realises Alagur isn't in his camp. You *DO* know how to ride, right?" Jymar says.

Alagur nods and proves he can by climbing on top of his wolf Yalla. All three men are visibly impressed by the boy's skill when they see it. Jymar takes the lead, and Jervis nods at Alagur to follow the man. He and Delgrun ride behind the boy.

Their journey's destination is half a morning away.

On arrival, Jymar will take the boy into the cave they use for their discussions whenever he and his men don't want any other Wolf Rider to know what they say. Today, the plan is to make sure this boy is as ready as they can make him for life as a Wolf Rider in under a day. Only Jymar knows the real reason for the actions. Belduran instructed him the boy is 'very important for the future of the Wolf Riders'. Jymar doesn't ask why. He accepts the command as fact and does what's asked of him.

Usually, he doesn't indulge himself with the demeaning activities that come after every attack on a city. But this time, it's different. However, he refrains from drinking alcohol to keep his senses.

Jymar leads his wolf into the cave.

"Bring your wolf, too. *No one* should see you're here," he says.

Alagur nods, and wonders where 'here' really was, or why he is in this place for that matter...

CHAPTER SIXTEEN

Alagur stares at his surroundings. He expected a damp, dark cave, but this place almost seems to be have been turned into a place to command an army from.

"You can direct the wolf to lie *there*," Jymar points at a part of the cave floor covered with thick leather hides, where Jymar's wolf is making himself comfortable at that moment. Alagur signals Yalla, and she lies in the same place, though some distance from the other wolves there.

Though older now, Yalla is still adjusting to a life among men, boys and many other wolves. Alagur can hear her whimper but gives her the signal to be silent. He looks around the cave once more. It's apparent from the way the walls are carved, that it was much smaller in the beginning.

His eyes see the markings of stone carving tools, which he recognises from the work he remembers his father doing.

Was one of these men a son of a stone carver once?

The work done in this cave shows military precision; it shows these men mean to go into battle against an adversary that's more extensive than just the townspeople of the nearby city to attack.

"Impressive, isn't it?" Jymar says, "It took forty of us a month to build all this…"

"Why am I here?" Alagur asks, "Why are you showing me this…?"

"They brought you here, because of me asking for you…"

Alagur spins around and stares into the faces of Belduran and

Vaymaz, standing side by side.

"Who's Samur?" Alagur asks, "Why is he in the city?"

"You miss little, boy, and if Vaymaz and I tell you this, these men all need to leave you with just us. When we've told you, you must bury this knowledge so deep, that not even facing a hundred wild wolves in the pit, will make you reveal it until it is the right time, and to the correct person," Vaymaz says.

"There's much more going on than you can even comprehend. It's not a coincidence you're among us, young Alagur," Belduran says, "Your coming, is part of the destiny of us all…"

"Why?" Alagur shouts, "I wanted to have a life with my father and mother, and my younger sister…"

"You're going to see them again one day," Belduran says, "But now we talk first…"

Alagur watches as all the Wolf Riders exit the cave. After just a few minutes, he's alone with the two Elder Men.

"Who are you?" he asks angrily.

"We're two of the Elder Men, who haven't trusted the one who snatched you, then brought you to City of Wolves," Vaymaz says, "… your destiny is for it all to stop… like it was prophesied so long ago…"

"Do all of them know?" Alagur screams and points at the cave exit, "Do *they* know about this… this… plan you got?"

"Not yet, though *one* has been told some, their role in the events will come. Has anyone already told you the words of *The Truth*?" Vaymaz asks gently.

"What's this thing called The Truth?" Alagur asks, but now the emotions welling up in him are causing him to cry.

"I'll tell you only the most important words right now. Those, that you must guard well," Vaymaz says, "But also those tied to your own destiny… and that of another, about whom you'll find out, of whom it's not safe to speak until much later…"

Alagur pauses and looks confused rather than angry for several minutes. Then he decides…

"Tell me, and I'll use the information to make sure I'm safe," he says.

Vaymaz and Belduran look at one for a moment, then each recites one verse of The Truth to the boy.

> Ten thousand riders rose to the call,
> Beset on to the city of old, and
> Fall before them it would.

> They who resisted would fall, and
> And young ones taken by force,
> And a city was lost to time and kin.

> For the Brothers betrayed truth, and
> Released fear upon the world,
> With wolves as their weapon.

> For legend foretells of their end,
> The end that will come from one,
> A brother who rises to the call.

Here, there's a pause in the recitation.

Alagur feels both men's eyes focused on him, and he wonders if there's a significance between the words just spoken, and their plans for him…

> The truth will show the doubter,
> He and his wolf will travel far,
> An agent of truth will show him.

> She whose name is unspoken,
> A wolf she will claim from the wild,
> And the man will learn her skill.

> Together they end the broken world,
> Heal the world to what it was before,
> It is that destiny that is unspoken.

Alagur stares at the two men when the echo of the last words fades from the cave.

"That's about the Wolf Riders?" Alagur asks.

"It *is*... and much more," Vaymaz says. "There are things we cannot tell you until you're much older, but remember this... do *NOT* trust the brother who came to the city filled with *lies*. He'd betray you as easily as he betrayed his own blood. I cannot tell you what I mean with those words, but I hope I can explain it one day..."

Alagur nods, and then he looks at the ground for a few moments and then looks up at the two men again.

"I'm ready. You can ask them to come back in, and for you and them to teach me everything that I need to know that is going to help me," Alagur says, "First lesson you can answer, is to explain to me the meaning of a recent dream I had of a girl with yellow hair and this strange necklace she wears... and her eyes. They're always black in this dream..."

Vaymaz and Belduran look visibly shaken by the words. Alagur sees this.

"Have told anyone else of this dream?" Belduran asks.

"No. I thought people laugh about it," Alagur answers.

"Recite again to me the fourth and fifth verses of The Truth," Belduran says in a stern voice.

Alagur did what he's told to do.

"Now, think about the words, and about what you just asked us," Vaymaz says, "If you listen *well* to those words, all of them, then it will answer every dream you'll have between now and when it's going to happen…"

"It's no coincidence you dreamt about her. She's part of the prophecy *too*, even if she isn't yet aware of it," Belduran says, "She'll have entered the prophecy herself *only* recently. Mark my words, Alagur, in half a decade from now, when you've almost forgotten all we've spoken of today, then you must set in motion what the of The Truth says…"

"A thousand years have passed since they were spoken," Vaymaz says, "It will in your lifetime, they'll have meaning. I won't be here to see it come to pass. I'm certain of it. But the hand, who deals my last moment, is tied to this prophecy, as much as those who want to see it come to pass…"

Alagur stares at the Elder Man, uncertain what to make of the words. He nods to show he understands…

"Let's begin, I have a lot to learn if I'm going to protect the wolf from him…"

CHAPTER SEVENTEEN

"Again…"

Alagur picks the spear arrow off the floor, and after a moment rushes towards Delgrun, who has taken it upon himself to teach the boy skills requiring to charge at an opponent. Delgrun allows the boy to charge at him, but leans sideways just enough to give the boy a taste of humility.

"Again…"

Alagur looks at Delgrun a moment and charges, but this time he sees the man swaying left, so at the last moment, moves the spear arrow in the man's direction's right side. There's an audible thud, and an equally audible letting out of expelled breath, and then a moment later, the man sits in the cave's dirt laughing.

Delgrun bends over and looks at the boy in surprise, breathing deep and often.

"Where did you learn *that?*" he asks between inhales of breath.

"I saw an ailep hound switch direction, so I changed direction."

"You *killed* an ailep hound?" Delgrun asks.

"Yes, I did. It was trailing me on the way to get Yalla…"

"Yalla?" Delgrun asks, "Is that what you named your wolf?"

Alagur swallows hard. He expects to be punished for naming the wolf before the Wolf Naming Ceremony, but none of such action came.

"Good name. She'll be brave in the battles that come your way,"

Delgrun says, "… *you* go tell Jymar that I think you're ready for the next exercise of learning…"

Alagur nods, then races towards the cave opening. He exits the cave and finds Jymar surrounded by eight of his men.

"Delgrun says I am ready for the next exercise of learning…"

"He did, didn't he?" Jymar says, "Good…"

Jymar gets up and stretches. "I guess I get to teach *you* how to use a sling. That's my mastery…" He laughs at the odd expression on the boy's face. "What's wrong?" he asks.

"I thought Wolf Riders only used spear arrows and rode their wolves," Alagur feels embarrassed suddenly.

"Don't be embarrassed. Most boys don't get past a year of learning. But we… that's Delgrun, Jervis and I, and a few others among my men I trust the most," Jymar explains, "We *all* have to teach to you in a few days, weeks, months what most boys would take a half-decade to learn."

Jymar pauses, then he speaks again. "He hasn't told me everything, but I'm not stupid. There's something Belduran means to do, and I feel that you, me, all of us *here* are a part of it. So, treat this as some of the most important days of your life," Jymar continues, "And don't worry about Samur. Between my men, who stayed behind, and Vaymaz, and Rudrig, we'll keep *that* runt Samur so drunk with heavy ales he won't miss you for weeks. But all those who do this, are risking much…"

"Why don't you or Belduran or some of the others not trust him?"

"Because, he bought is way into our midst with betrayal of an innocent man, that some in City of Wolves claim to be his father…"

Alagur spins around when he hears the newcomer's voice. As a silhouette against the sharp daylight beyond, Alagur sees Rudrig standing there.

"I came to see how he's progressing here," Rudrig says.

"He's doing well. He's smart, patient, and strong. All good qualities a Wolf Rider must possess," Jymar says, "I'll have to teach sling throwing still, then he'll be ready for the wolf test…"

Alagur looks back at Jymar. "Wolf test?" he asks. "What wolf test?"

"In a bonding with a wolf, it must be complete or else in the heat of battle a wolf can abandon a Wolf Rider when he needs such a person the most…" Jymar explains.

"But I'm already bonded with her…"

"We know, but tradition dictates it…" Jymar says, then adds in a gentler voice, "It will make the bond even stronger…"

"And I can do this test because you made me ready?"

"Yes, but Belduran thinks you attracted undue attention with your wolf, which is *why* you didn't get prepared for the wolf test by him," Jymar says.

"I was warned about him," Alagur says, with an edge of caution to his own voice.

"All I'll say is that it was with good reason," Jymar says, "These are dangerous times, Alagur, *more* dangerous than you know or realise. But one day, you must make a choice. Belduran, Rudrig and Vaymaz, and none of us will stand in the way of that choice, but whatever you decide, can have a greater impact than you know right now…"

Alagur nods and silently considers the words. *I already thought about leaving. Perhaps all this is to make sure I can do that…*

He keeps what he's thinking to himself. To those Wolf Riders around him, who see him every day, the expression is of someone sullen and moody. Only some among the men realise there are likely other reasons for the change in his mood. Even fewer will later realise, he had been plotting his departure, because of words were spoken to him by those who want the days of the Wolf Riders to end. He trains for several days more, then does the wolf test, which seems very easy in his mind. He's silently returned to the encampment just a day or so before they're for return to the City of Wolves. Because of what's done in his absence, most don't realise he returned after a period of absence, organised in secret by those with their own plans for the future.

He develops a routine with the wolf. He wakes up, then brushes the wolf over, and readies the animal for riding, and when the thousands there ride that day to get back to the city, he's one of those who rides with them. But in learning more about the life he's forced into when he got snatched, he plans his departure now.

The opportunity will come some five years later, and he will even orchestrate the *same* for a boy he'll meet just months before it happened…

Alagur feels disappointed when finally they ride back through the old gatehouse which once served as a secure entrance for the ancient city. An hour later, he's in the small courtyard next to his dwelling, and busies himself with untying the harness he used on his wolf, and then stands to brush his wolf over.

Samur arrives an hour later, and Alagur glances at the man, and to him, it feels the man stands to scrutinise each of his actions by staring at him from just a short distance.

He wonders what Samur might be thinking, but decides not to ask.

This settles into a routine over the next few weeks and months, which is only interrupted by the occasional excursions from the city to attack another city as a victim of the Wolf Riders.

It will be half a decade later when the purpose of the routine becomes more apparent…

CHAPTER EIGHTEEN

Samur tells Alagur one morning, "I've got plans for *that* wolf…"

Alagur laughs about the idea. Although he laughs off the words so regularly, he feels almost like the man is plunging a spear arrow into his back.

I don't know what you have got planned, but you stay away from my wolf.

Alagur glances at Samur while drinking hot tea. It has been a year now since the encounter in the cave, and at his fifteen years old, he's more mature than most. He heeds the words of caution every day…

Alagur pays attention to everything that goes on in the city. He notices Samur behaves in the way he'd been told about, and Alagur feels the need to be more cautious around him, especially when an unknown man arrives with Samur a few weeks later.

Alagur doesn't see the Elder Men, who'd spoken those the words of caution, much; they seem to avoid contact, mostly, to make sure the boy doesn't get into any danger it seems. He meets Jymar a few times, and it's mostly a routine to meet to learn more skills. During this time, the man asks Alagur more about Chiva'na, though memories of his birth city are becoming a blur for Alagur, who admits he doesn't remember much of it because he had left the city as a boy. But the one vivid memory he still holds onto is that of a young girl calling out to him.

"Alagur, Alagur…"

Samur behaves like he's a friend to the boy, but something about his behaviour makes him think it's all just pretence. Alagur still thinks of him as a friend, but there's a measure of distrust for the man growing in his heart. Each day, he sees more evidence that proves he isn't alone in this distrust.

However, when Samur talks more about establishing a squad, Alagur wants to believe him, but will often laugh off the idea. He sees Yalla and Uzo have grown close over the preceding time, though his hand signals add pretence to this and in reality it's obvious his wolf favours another wolf more; Alagur pretends to believe that the words are true. He'll pretend to be Samur's friend until he knows more of what the man plans to do.

Then the changes are apparent.

Samur is more abrupt in his behaviour and will swing from being extremely caring and friendly to days where he'll beat up the boy. But Alagur practises what he'd learnt from Jymar and others daily, and knows his fists grow stronger.

Initially, he takes out his frustration on boys younger than himself; beating them to vent the frustration he feels from being bullied by a man who's supposed to be a friend. The day it changes is when he counters Samur's hand with a counterpunch. This angers Samur, but the man realises he can no longer beat Alagur to submission after that.

From that day, Alagur sees the man walk off at a fast pace, and doesn't know what the man does while he's gone. And then, as nothing has happened, Samur will arrive back grinning, and waving a pitcher filled with a wine of some sort towards him. Alagur gets into a routine after that himself…

He will greet Samur as nothing has happened with a *"Hail, Samur"*.

This became routine in the years that followed…

Alagur notices fast, that Samur drinks a lot of wine or ale, and he'll sleep until well after the middle of the day arrives. He notices disdain from other Wolf Riders for this behaviour.

But today, Alagur has become the object of a beating once more.

Rather than accepting it, he hits back, and Samur sits glaring at him for a time before he gets up and walks off. Alagur glares at the man walking away at a fast pace. It's the first time, in all the time he'd been in City of Wolves, he feels hatred, seething almost uncontrollable hatred, towards Samur.

Something about the man's behaviour isn't right. Edgryn had been right all along, and he paid a heavy price for the warning. They found his body in a side alley just three days earlier, his neck snapped in two, where someone used excessive force to kill him. The body stank of ale, so it's assumed by most he got in a brawl with another drunkard, and they fought, and in the brawl, the unimaginable happened.

Such occurrences are frequent in the City of Wolves…

But his words of caution, that he spoke to a boy who earned his respect, were his undoing. It makes Alagur much more cautious from that day onward.

It will be the cautious nature which, one late winter morning, will set a new destiny in motion for him as a man.

But there are too many days, weeks, months, and years to go through before it happens.

It's a hard lesson that he, Alagur, will one day pass on to a much younger boy…

THE END

Here's how to keep in touch with me!

My website   **nathaliemlromer.com**

Twitter   twitter.com/nmlromer
Facebook   facebook.com/nathaliemlromer
Blog   nathaliemlromer.blog
GoodReads   goodreads.com/nathaliemlromer
Bookbub   bookbub.com/authors/nathalie-m-l-romer

"Thank you so much for reading my book. I hope
it will give you many more years of enjoyment."

Nathalie M.L. Römer

ABOUT THE AUTHOR

Nathalie M.L. Römer was born in the Netherlands, lived there during her childhood before she moved to Curaçao as a teenager. From there, she then moved to Britain to live there for twenty-five years, before moving to Sweden where she now lives with her partner Anders.

In her childhood years and beyond, Nathalie has always loved to read novels. In her local library as a child, she would often borrow "adult audience" science fiction and fantasy novels, and as the bookworm, that she was (and still is), she would read them all in a few days... and go back for more, often. The genres that interest Nathalie the most are science fiction, fantasy and historical novels. Her favourite authors include various science fiction, fantasy fiction and historical fiction authors that include (but are not limited to) Isaac Asimov, Richard A. Knaak, Jean M. Auel, and Christie Golden.

In addition, to reading novels, the other interests she pursues include needlework and crafts, archaeology, reading about various science topics, home cooking, photography, web design, and playing MMO games - mostly World of Warcraft which Nathalie credits as having directly inspired her to write stories.

About the wolves in this novella!

Some aspects of how a wolf behaves in this story, have been fictionalised to fit in with the fantasy setting of the novel, however I've done much research into how these beautiful animals behave in their natural environment and around humans and drawing on experiences as a dog owner, to create Yalla - who is the primary wolf to feature in the story. I base some of her mannerisms on an Alsatian I used to own, while I also have tried to capture how a wolf could behave in nature.

Please support the various wolf sanctuary charities that exist to give this misunderstood animal the credit it deserves!